# THE ROPE LADDER

D1431190

Other books by Nigel Richardson

*The Wrong Hands*

# THE ROPE LADDER

## NIGEL RICHARDSON

OXFORD
UNIVERSITY PRESS

# OXFORD
UNIVERSITY PRESS

Great Clarendon Street, Oxford OX2 6DP

Oxford University Press is a department of the University of Oxford.
It furthers the University's objective of excellence in research, scholarship,
and education by publishing worldwide in

Oxford New York

Auckland Cape Town Dar es Salaam Hong Kong Karachi
Kuala Lumpur Madrid Melbourne Mexico City Nairobi
New Delhi Shanghai Taipei Toronto

With offices in

Argentina Austria Brazil Chile Czech Republic France Greece
Guatemala Hungary Italy Japan Poland Portugal Singapore
South Korea Switzerland Thailand Turkey Ukraine Vietnam

Oxford is a registered trade mark of Oxford University Press
in the UK and in certain other countries

First published 2007

British Library Cataloguing in Publication Data
Data available

ISBN: 978-0-19-271977-5

1 3 5 7 9 10 8 6 4 2

Typeset in Sabon by TnQ Books and Journals Pvt. Ltd.,
Chennai, India

Printed in Great Britain
by Cox & Wyman Ltd, Reading Berkshire

In memory of two friends and fathers
Christopher Gilbert
1950–2004
Tim Petter
1959–2006

# Chapter 1

I stood in front of the wolf enclosure and a wolf soon appeared, following the line of the fence. It looked ungainly at first. It had its head down and its thin white legs moved stiffly and awkwardly. But that was deceptive. A wolf only shows about five per cent of what it is capable of. The rest is hidden until it needs it. Soon this wolf showed more interest. As it came near me it lifted its head and speeded up into a springy, elastic trot. Its fur was thick and swirling in shades of white and brown, like the froth on cappuccino.

It looked as if it was smiling. It was panting with its mouth open and its tongue was furled like a slice of ham between the daggers of its lower teeth. But it wasn't smiling. Wolves don't smile at humans. Normally they don't even bother looking at us, because humans are boring to a wolf. There are too many of us, we all look the same, and we do the same things, such as stop and stare at them, and click our fingers, and make growling noises. Then we walk off, back to our human lives that can never be remotely enviable to a wolf.

But I didn't do those things. I stood dead still and concentrated, trying to talk to it with my mind. And

1

the wolf looked at me. Admittedly it showed no more interest in me than I would show in a sweet wrapper I saw on the pavement. But still, for a fraction of a second it did look at me. Its smoky yellow eyes glowed as if there was a fire burning behind them, a fire in the centre of the wolf's head. Those eyes communicated things. I couldn't tell you exactly what things because they were wolf-thoughts, and they don't translate brilliantly into human thoughts, but I felt them.

Sometimes the wolf-thoughts calmed me down and sometimes they wound me up. That day, they calmed me down. I needed calming down. Ten minutes before, I'd beaten a kid up really badly and the feel of him was still buzzing on my fists. I didn't beat him up on my own, mind. I don't just mean that my mates, Vernon Crottall and Barry Lunc, were involved too. I mean there was something inside me that took over and made me do it even though I didn't want to. It had never happened to me before and it was scary.

Mum got to know about it, but at the same time she didn't know about it at all. She saw my swollen face, and the dried blood I didn't realize was hanging out of one nostril, and jumped to the wrong conclusion: that I'd been the victim of a random, unprovoked attack by one of the hundreds of lip-ringed nutters she reckoned roamed the Lock area. She may even have been pleased in a funny way, because it was an added reason to move out of London.

'We can't leave soon enough, if you ask me,' she said. 'You'll love it in the country, love, I promise.

We'll get away from all this madness.' She didn't know that the madness was *me*.

Regent's Canal towpath, between Camden Lock and Regent's Park, an afternoon in July. Vern, Barry, and I had gone down there with some cans of cider. It's true, you get a lot of weirdos shuffling past—bag-ladies with tangerine hair, paedos with Stanley knives in their back pockets—but we could handle it, we were Camden. We were sitting on the bench where the nar-rowboats tie up. The boat directly in front of us, called *Bilbo Baggins*, was twee as you like with flowers painted round the windows. Its curtains were closed except for one window where there was a tiny gap that you could probably have seen through if you went right up to the boat and knelt down. Vern said that maybe there was a woman in the boat getting undressed. He dared me to go and have a look but I wouldn't. We carried on watching people walking by on the towpath and laughing at the divvy ones. For instance, a bar code went by—that's a balding bloke who tries to disguise it by brushing thin strands of hair over the bald patch—followed by a gaggle of what Vern called cancer slags: fat women in too-tight leg-gings, smoking snouts.

And I was thinking to myself how sound Barry and Vern were. When we met we used to do this thing of interlocking our arms and fingers and squeezing really hard while banging our foreheads together and

3

frowning. We'd got it from a new goal celebration that the Arsenal players had started doing.

This is how weird Mum could be: she didn't like Barry but she thought Vern was OK. Dad once had a go at her about it. It was after she'd said she didn't want me going to a party at Barry's house because his mum wasn't going to be there, it was just his elder brother in charge of all these twelve-year-old boys.

Dad said, 'Be honest, Clare, you're just finding excuses. You don't like the lad and that's what it's about.'

'I don't *not* like him,' Mum said. 'I just don't trust his brother to act responsibly.'

'Why not?' said Dad. 'How old is he, kidder?' (Kidder was what Dad called me, when he wasn't using my real name. That's a lot better than Mong, which is what Vern and some others called me sometimes, or Slimehead, on account of my lack of earlobes.)

'About twenny,' I said.

'Sounds plenny old enough to me,' he said, 'to keep ten pre-pubescent toerags in check.'

'Cheers for that,' I said. It was good fun being insulted by Dad.

'What's he doing living at home at twenty-odd?' Mum said.

'Cos he can't afford the bloody rents in this high-stakes metropolis of ours,' said Dad.

'Because he's signing on and taking drugs,' said Mum. 'And teaching the youngsters dangerous tricks on their mountain bikes. What's he doing mucking about on bikes at his age?'

4

Mum is quite right-wing, by the way.

'Oh, and what about Barry's mum while we're about it?' Dad said.

'What about her?' said Mum.

'The truth is, Clare, you like Vernon Crottall because his mum is a GP in Highgate and his dad's on the news, and you don't like Barry whatsisname—'

'Lunc,' I said.

'Lunc because he hasn't got a live-in dad and his mum is—what is she, kidder?'

'An out-reach worker for Camden Council.'

I almost said something, except I didn't want to sneak on my friends. But the point was, if Mum only knew what a nutter Vern was, with his quack mother and his foreign-correspondent-on-the-telly-in-a-flak-jacket dad. It was Vern who got me to lick a beer can that had been in the freezer. It was Vern who nicked a McDonald's cup full of coins from a tramp with a baseball bat outside Chalk Farm tube. It was Vern who smoked drugs at thirteen and nicked money out of his mum's purse and condoms out of his dad's laptop bag and tried to persuade Barry and me to go with him to pick up a prostitute behind King's Cross station. And it was Vern who decided it would be a brilliant idea to roll that kid who came past as we sat on the bench by the canal that afternoon, drinking cider, and I was staring into space thinking what a sound couple of mates I had, and how I was going to miss them when we moved out of London.

I knew the kid. He was a bit mental, used to hang out around Camden Lock, just standing there nodding his head most of the time although sometimes he was paid about 5p a day to hand out leaflets advertising a tattoo and piercing studio called The Damage Done. I remembered him because a couple of weeks before he'd gobbed on my trainer. Deliberately. I was waiting at a foodstall to get a cardboard plate of fish balls and noodles and, bam, out it came, a horrible stringy one that stayed in the air so my trainer and his mouth were joined for a second by a suspension bridge of yellow gob. He was looking at it, nodding at it, then he said, 'Posh twat,' and walked off.

I wasn't at a posh school. It was a comprehensive, although not the same comprehensive as the Gobber. In our school quite a lot of kids' parents were like mine: OK off but not ra-ra rich. Ra-ra rich was having a daddy who wore a suit and drove a Bentley and sent you to a boarding school where they wore uniforms that hadn't changed for about three hundred years. Ra-ra dads didn't wear a leather waistcoat and crêpe-soled George Cox leopardskin creepers, bought from the Doc Marten shop round the corner from Camden tube. My parents just happened to be quite cool, or Dad was anyway. But the Gobber still hated me, or people who looked like me. And I hated the Gobber, not just because he gobbed on my trainer (my mum had to put it in the washing machine, and then it was bleached out so she had to put the other one in too to even them up) but because he made me be too much of a coward to do anything back to him.

I admit I was probably a tiny bit pissed: I'd almost finished my can of Strongbow. But anyway, I saw this bloke coming along the towpath from Camden Lock direction. His head was down, he was walking in tiny little steps that made him look like a mong. I nudged Vern so we could laugh at him. Then I realized who it was: the Gobber. I put my hands out, one on Vern's arm, the other on Barry's so they'd know something was up and I wanted them to be quiet. And we watched as the Gobber walked past us. Then I made the mong noise, the grunting, chimp/cow/pig noise you make to mean someone's mental: *nur, nur, nuuurrrrr*. I thought it was going to be OK. The Gobber just carried on walking. Vern said, 'Who's that then?' and I said, 'Tell you later.'

But then the Gobber stopped. He didn't turn round at first, he stopped walking but carried on facing ahead, towards the park, his head nodding slightly. I thought, Oh shit. Then I thought, But I'll be OK. I've got Vern and Barry with me. Oh yeah?

The Gobber turned round and walked back till he was in front of the bench. He still had his head down, as if he was looking for something tiny he'd dropped in the mud (his brain, for instance). He didn't make eye contact but he said, from under his hair, 'Who made that noise?' In other circumstances this would have been funny, because his voice was very similar to the chimp/cow/pig noise he was complaining of. But I wasn't laughing and neither were Vern or Barry. In fact, what Vern and Barry were doing was sliding

7

away from me along the bench so it was just me left on my own in the middle. And it was obvious who made the noise.

I wanted to slide left or right too, so I wasn't sitting on my own. I felt stupid and exposed sitting there, not saying anything, with the Gobber standing right in front of me, also not saying anything, and not looking at me either, but just nodding his head as if he'd got a screw loose in his neck. It was an embarrassing and stupid moment that was soon stretching into loads of embarrassing and stupid moments and I knew already that Vern and Barry were going to give me a hard time about it afterwards, for starting something I couldn't finish, for making the mong noise and not knowing where to go with it.

I noticed the Gobber's trainers and they made me feel sad because they were cardboard-looking and I knew they sold them in bins outside shoe shops in the high street for about seven quid. Somebody walked past behind the Gobber on the towpath. I wanted it to be a bossy adult who'd stick her big nose in and tell us all to get lost, and Vern, Barry, and I could scoot off to the park and stand outside the wolf enclosure looking for movement, looking for a flash of their yellow eyes that reminded me of the old-fashioned marbles you could buy at the Lock. But the person walked on and left us to it.

And then the Gobber did what he did best. Bam. He didn't need to look or take aim, he just lifted his chin and out spurted this horror-movie flame of stringy, yellowy gob. He may have been a nutter but he was a world-class gobber. It didn't land on my trainer this time. If only. It only landed on my head, that's all. But I didn't react. Inside my brain I was running round in circles with my arse on fire and a blue flashing light strapped to my head, yelling 'Gross' and 'Bastard' and 'Aaagghh'. But outside: nothing.

The Gobber had turned and was walking off towards the park. Maybe he'd already forgotten what had just happened. Maybe his brain was incredibly slow-working, like a dinosaur's, which was why he took so long to stop and come back to me after I made the noise I now really wished I hadn't made, because I was in a no-win situation and I knew Vern and Monster weren't going to let me forget this for a long time. Maybe for ever.

Barry produced a blubbery laugh, meaning he couldn't believe what he'd just seen. I felt the gob sliding down my hair and for a split-second I thought I might puke. I found some old toilet paper in my pocket and tried to wipe the gob off casually so my mates didn't see. But Vern did see. He said, 'Don't put that near me, he's probably HIV positive.' Then he shoved my arm and said, 'Go on then.'

'What?'

'Do him. He's getting away. Batter him. Push him in the canal. Whatever.'

'Nah. He's not worth it.'

Vern looked really angry. 'You're joking,' he said.

Barry said, 'Leave it out, Vern. If that's what he wants . . .'

9

'*I'll* do him then,' said Vern. And he stood up. 'D'you want me to do him, yeah?'

'No. Listen,' I said, 'let's just forget it, yeah? The guy's a mong. He doesn't know what he's doing.'

'He's getting away,' said Vern. He pointed down the towpath where, in the distance, the figure of the Gobber was still visible as he walked under a bridge. Vern was angry. 'Course he knows what he's doing. He didn't just like *accidentally* happen to gob on your head, did he? The bloke needs sorting out.'

'Let's go back to the Lock,' I said. 'Chill. Look at some CDs. I'll buy you a CD. Or vintage vinyl. You've got a record deck, haven't you?'

The story might have ended here, with three sound mates drifting back to the Lock to blow money on music. But, then, Vern made the comment and raised the subject that changed everything.

He said, 'Is it cos of your dad?'

Dad had died in the depth of winter. It had been nearly five months and Vern and Barry had never mentioned it, not since the day after it happened. 'What are you talking about?' I said. I wasn't angry, not immediately. It was more a feeling of numbness.

Vern wouldn't let it go. He said: 'Is it cos of your dad dying that you're wimping out? Is it cos of your dad dying that I'm not recognizing you as the sort of mate I would hang out with, who gets into heavy situations and can't handle it cos they've suddenly turned into a mong, you slime'ead mong?'

10

Now the anger kicked in. 'Piss off, Vern,' I said, and started running. Partly I was running so he and Barry couldn't see I was crying. Partly I was running because suddenly, more than anything, I wanted to see the wolves in Regent's Park zoo. Which meant I was running towards the park. Which meant I was running after the Gobber. You could tell I wasn't thinking straight.

Vern and Barry came after me. Vern caught up with me first and slapped me on the back as we ran. 'Go for it, yeah?' he said. He didn't understand what I was doing, why I was running. I had no intention of battering the Gobber. Except now I did. I had to, even though it wasn't what I wanted to do. How weird is life, that often you end up doing the last thing in the world you meant to do. Like moving to a deadsville village in the middle of the countryside, or attacking a poor kid with a dinosaur brain from behind.

I couldn't believe it but the Gobber didn't turn round when he heard our footsteps on the muddy towpath. All I could see was his back, a black bomber jacket stretched across it, and I was wondering what to do to it. Left and right, Vern and Barry were like a motorbike escort. But it was me, the politician in the middle, who had to do the business.

Even when I got right up behind the Gobber, so I could reach out and touch his shoulder, even then I didn't know what I was going to do. Then I saw his head move, his shoulder start to swing round, and I just did it, this stupid thing that must have looked pathetic if a CCTV camera had caught it, for instance—which was a possibility that freaked me for weeks afterwards. I sort of ran into the back of him with my elbows up but I didn't catch him clean because his body was just starting to turn. My elbows slid off him and I half tripped but managed to stay on my feet. The Gobber went down as I'd intended, but not for long. I hopped up and down as if I was skipping with an invisible rope as I watched him rolling in the mud. Then he bounced back up.

He didn't look at me, or not with his eyes anyway, but he knew where I was. He rushed me and I had nowhere to go. I wasn't going to run—even I wasn't that much of a wimp, at least if Vern and Barry were around—but I didn't know how to stop him. He was a dinosaur on go-faster pills.

I put my hands up to protect my face but he wasn't coming for me with his fists. He'd got one arm out and as he ran into my chest he swung the arm round my neck and brought my head down into a tight lock under his armpit. And in a flash I was sunk in this alien, armpit-and-bomber-jacket world, scratchily black and smelling of unwashed pits and washing that's been left too long in the washing machine. The upper half of my body was locked solid. I could hardly breathe never mind speak. Snot was coming out of my nose and I felt my eyes bulging. A sort of silent humming sounded in my covered ears.

Then the Gobber hit me in the face with his free fist. Bam bam. Twice. Intense heat on my nose, pain blipping

12

out to my ears. I twisted and turned, pushed up, pulled back. I hardly moved a centimetre. My entire head felt on fire. My ears were like barbs on a fish hook. The more I moved to free myself, the more they stuck in the lock of the Gobber's arms. Imagine if I'd had proper earlobes like everyone else (except Mum—that's who I got mine off). I'd still be down there, in the Gobber's armpit.

But the Eighth Armoured Division was on its way. There was a scuffle above and below me, arms thrashing about and feet losing their grip in the mud, and suddenly my ears were free. It was like coming up to the surface of a swimming pool. I could hear, I could make sense.

Vern and Barry were either side of the Gobber and they were pulling him off me. They were making noises that weren't quite words, like 'Oi, yuss now, watch it, fu—, shoot, jeez, ayee, ayee,' and then my whole body was free. A head that felt over-inflated. Ears stinging, eyes watering, and in my blurred vision, the Gobber. Vern and Barry were clamped on to either arm. He was standing there right in front of me with his head down, a captured dinosaur. We were all breathing heavily. Vern said, 'Go on then.'

'Wha—?' My mouth was so dry I couldn't speak properly.

'Do him. Knee him. Chop him. Whatever. But get on with it, for Christ's sake, we can't hold him all day.'

I looked to left and right. No one around. I looked back at the Gobber. And at that moment, inside me, something snapped.

* * *

Let's not go into detail, but I did what Vern said. I battered the Gobber. I battered him so badly that Vern and Barry shouted at me to stop. But I didn't stop, and they grabbed hold of me to try to make me. Then a woman in a house on the far side of the canal shouted that she was calling the police and, finally, I did stop. And we scattered. Or Vern, Barry, and I did. I'm not sure how well the Gobber could walk after what I did to him.

I thought my mates were running with me, but when I slowed down and looked back, they weren't there. I'd reached the park by then. My heart was fluttering and freaked, it felt like an injured bird I'd once held beneath my hands. I tried calling Vern on my mobile. No answer. I couldn't work out what had happened, where they'd gone. I was worried about what they'd think of me. Maybe they'd deliberately escaped from me, not wanting to associate with a maniac. Was I a maniac?

I stood outside the wolf enclosure, and soon that wolf appeared to beam some calmness back into me with its eyes. I pushed my stinging, buzzing fists deep in my pockets and regulated my breathing to the wolf's slow pant. How to explain what the wolf said to me that day? Something like: don't worry, doing one bad thing doesn't make you a bad person. Everyone does a bad thing now and again. You just happened to do yours today. And anyway, you've got a pretty good excuse for not being on top of your life at this present moment. It's not every fifteen-year-old kid whose dad decides to croak on him.

*Calma, calma*, as Dad used to say. I breathed deeply and closed my eyes. When I opened them, the wolf had disappeared down its tunnel, job done.

The calmness lasted till I left the park to walk back to Gloucester Crescent. Then the human world rushed back into my head and flew around it like a flock of panicking birds. How badly had I injured the Gobber? Maybe he was an asthmatic and had had an attack and died. It happened. Had the police been called? If he was still alive, would he be able to give the police a proper description of the three kids who'd jumped him on the towpath? What about the woman in the house on the other side of the canal? How good a view had she got? Where had Vern and Barry gone? Maybe they'd gone to the police themselves to shop me because I was an out-of-control maniac. What about CCTV? It was everywhere, CCTV. It must have captured me. I imagined seeing me on *Crimewatch*, the blurry film of a kid battering another kid followed by the request to come forward if you think you recognize the batterer. (Step forward half of Camden Town and Chalk Farm.)

I was going to tell Mum what had happened, what I'd done. I wasn't going to shift the blame, either. Even the Gobber gobbing on me didn't excuse what I had done. Even Vern being a shit-stirrer. I was going to tell her everything so she could know that her son was a maniac. But she didn't give me the chance. When I opened the front door she was in the hallway, crouched

15

down in front of the cupboard under the stairs. There was a box there and a bin bag and she was transferring stuff from the box to the bin bag. I knew straight away it was Dad's stuff because she was crying.

'Sorry,' she said, as if it was a crime to cry. She wiped her nose with the back of her hand and gave a big sniff. 'What have you been up to? Have you had a nice time?' Then she tensed up, staring at me. I didn't realize what I looked like, that I had dried blood hanging from one nostril, my face was red and swollen, and my knuckles were raw and bloody. 'Oh, love,' she said. I hated myself then. I wasn't a love, I was a maniac.

She got up, ran towards me and hugged me, squeezing me nearly as tightly as the Gobber. She smelt of the scented drawers where she kept her silk kimonos. She didn't speak and I didn't speak, and then I knew the moment had gone when I could tell her what really happened. Call it a wolf-thought, but I knew the right moment—the only moment—had gone. Her tears soaked my shirt. 'Oh, love,' she said again, and her breath tickled the hairs on my neck. Then she pushed me away, held me at arm's length and stared in my eyes. 'Who did this to you?'

I looked away. 'Just a kid. I got him back.' I held up my bloody knuckles, and she hugged me again, for being brave. (Hah!)

She took me into the downstairs bathroom and wiped my nose with cotton wool and that was when I saw what a state I was in and she talked about the move we were about to make, how I would love it in the country and how London was no place to bring up kids. And I didn't say anything but she didn't think that was out of order. If you've just been attacked by a bully who is much bigger and stronger than you, for no reason, you don't feel like talking much, do you?

The next morning I was woken by someone banging on the front door, so loudly it made my bedroom windows shake even though they were on the third floor. First thing I did was remember what had happened the day before. Second thing was to be shit-scared about the banging on the door. It was what the police did. They probably had a bloke at the front with a battering ram, and about twenty of them were lined up behind him in riot gear, ready to storm the house looking for the juvenile maniac who'd battered an asthmatic with special needs to death on the canal towpath near Camden Lock the previous afternoon.

I jumped out of bed and went to the window. But there were no police vehicles parked along the street, there was just a motorbike belonging to a courier company right outside our door. And downstairs in the kitchen, a despatch rider in leathers was drinking coffee from the Arsenal mug while Mum signed legal papers to do with Dad's will that needed to be returned straight away to the solicitor.

I bought the *Camden New Journal* and the *Hampstead and Highgate Express*, looking for the story. Nothing. After three days of texting and leaving voicemails I got through to Vern. He said he was in Suffolk for a week staying in his parents' cottage. We didn't talk about what had happened. He sounded different, as if he didn't want to be talking to me. I knew then I had a whiff of weirdness on me. A wolf, for instance, would back off if it met me. But the weirdness wasn't just to do with the battering I'd given the Gobber, the trapdoor I had opened on myself in those mad moments by the canal. That was bad enough, but there was something else. Dad dying had left us with no choice but to downsize. Mum and I were going to move house—away from Camden, out of London—and that was like being given a death sentence. If Vern and Barry never saw me again, which was possible, it would be no different from if I was dead. So I wasn't just a dangerous batterer of defenceless mongs, I was terminally ill as well. No wonder Vern was reluctant to talk to me.

Before Vern finished the call I said, 'When we move to the country will you come down and stay with us, you and Monster Mash? I'm going to be bored out of my skull down there.'

'Yeah. Whatever.' Translation: no way, Jose.

Me getting beaten up (i.e., Mum's version of what happened) made Mum speed up all the arrangements to move. She said it was the final straw; she didn't want to be in London a second longer than absolutely necessary. The house in Gloucester Crescent was already on the market for £1.5 million, but Mum said we'd be lucky to see fifty grand of that after Dad's debts had been paid off. Meanwhile we had a ready-made place to move to because Mum's parents, my grandma and grandpa, had both died the year before, leaving Mum their cottage in the village that time forgot. This also happened to be the house that Mum grew up in back when she wore plaits (I've seen the evidence) and played the middle of a pantomime centipede in a play in the village hall.

The day before Mum and I left Gloucester Crescent for ever, I called Vern and Barry and told them I wouldn't be around any more after today and how about meeting up. We hadn't seen each other since the incident with the Gobber.

We met outside Out On the Floor Records in Inverness Street and walked down by the canal to the park. We walked past the bench we'd been sitting on, we walked past the place where it had happened. But we didn't say one word about the day I went crazy. In fact we hardly spoke. It was as if I was on my deathbed and they were sitting around wondering what to say, staring out of the hospital window and wishing they were anywhere but where they were, watching a kid who used to be a mate, but wasn't any more, about to pop his clogs.

We stood outside the wolf enclosure and I did some wolf-thoughts to get a wolf to come out and look at us, but no wolf appeared. Then Vern said he had to go because he was meeting his mum in Tottenham Court Road so she could buy him an i-Pod, and Barry said he was going to catch the bus with Vern. We did the Arsenal goal celebration thing, there and then, in Regent's Park, on the footpath outside the wolf enclosure. Except it wasn't a celebration. Then Vern and Barry walked out of my life. And I did the same. I turned my back on the Regent's Park wolves and walked out of my own life.

# Chapter 2

Deadsville, early August. It took us less than two hours to get there. Whizzing out of London on a dual carriageway that widened into a motorway, Mum was going, 'Ah, sanity' and 'What a relief' and stuff like that. I didn't say anything because we were leaving Dad behind and that didn't feel like sanity (Dad's ashes are scattered on Hampstead Heath).

When we reached the driveway of the cottage, which was called 'The Hollow' (puke), Mum lifted on the handbrake, turned the ignition off, and sat there, not moving, not speaking, staring through the windscreen. The engine made a ticking sound as it cooled down. In front of the car was a trellis with roses growing up it and beyond that the garden. A bench, a watering can, grass that needed cutting. Mum was staring at the garden but she wasn't seeing it. She was seeing her future, that's what I reckoned, because I was doing the same thing. I was staring at a coil of hosepipe mounted on the garage wall and thinking, This is it. No sound, no noise at all. I strained my ears and they finally tuned into a bird singing. The bird was singing 'Welcome to Deadsville'.

Mum brought the sides of her hands down on the steering wheel and said, 'Hey ho.'

And I said, 'I hate trees, I hate fresh air, and I particularly have it in for blinking bluebells.'


This was a family joke. We visited the cottage quite a lot when Grandma and Grandpa were alive. Once, Dad and I went for a walk to the magic barn, so he could get away from what he called Gran's wittering for half an hour. To get there we walked through a bluebell wood and I thought it was surprisingly nice, considering. Considering Dad had always said the countryside was crap. At one point we had to clamber over fallen branches covered in moss. The sun was shining through the trees in fans of light and landing on the moss so it looked like the greenest green you've ever seen. A queen in a fairytale would have jewel boxes lined with moss like that (don't tell Tally I said that, she'd think I was a secret girl).The sunlight was also landing on the bluebells covering the floor of the wood. Dad's leopardskin creepers, that Grandma hated so much, were ploughing through a sea of purple-blue flowers.

We carried on towards the barn, which was on the top of a flat hill. It was 'magic' because it made brilliant echoes, throwing your voice back really loud a split-second after you had shouted. As we walked towards it I turned to Dad and said, 'Iss all right out 'ere, innit?' in a jokey street-cred voice, but still meaning what I said, and Dad said, 'No, I hate it. I hate trees, I hate fresh air, and I particularly have it in for blinking bluebells.'

He started to stamp up and down like a maniac, shouting, 'What do we want? Tattoo parlours and record stores. When do we want them? Now!'

And the magic barn shouted back, 'NOW! NOW! NOW!'

Mum dumped a couple of shopping bags on the kitchen work surface, then went through into the living room and slumped in the armchair that used to be Grandma's. The ceilings were low in The Hollow. The light was gloomy and depressing. There was a smell of damp and cobwebs full of dead flies hung in the corners of the window. Mum put her head in her hands and said, 'Horrid flies.' Then, forcing a smile, she patted the arms of the chair and said, 'Be a love and put the kettle on.'

I went through to the kitchen and made two mugs of tea. When I took Mum's back through she was crying. 'Thanks, love,' she said. 'You're a good boy. An amazing boy really. Eh?'

I thought, No, I'm a kid-battering maniac. But I said, 'What's the matter?'

'Oh, nothing. It's just an emotional day, that's all. The first day of the rest of our lives.'

She said it sarcastically but I knew that she meant it. Except she hardly got the word 'lives' out because she had started crying again. I said, 'D'you want to talk about it?'

Mum laughed even though she was crying. 'You've really grown up, haven't you, these last few weeks? Well, it's like this. I've been looking forward to this day. I thought, the moment we stepped through that front door'—she pointed over her shoulder—'we'd be fine. Clean sheet. Start again. But life's not like that, I'm afraid.' She blew her nose. 'I'm sorry, love. I shouldn't burden you with this. You've got your own life to worry about. It's just . . . difficult sometimes. Without your father.'

'Can I go back up to London sometimes to see him?'

'What do you mean?'

'Just go for a walk on the Heath. And I can talk to Dad in my head. Then maybe I can see Vern and Barry.'

'Of course you can. I've told you. It's only an hour from the nearest station to Waterloo. Then straight up the Northern line. It's not Outer Mongolia, you know.'

'Feels like it,' I said. 'Gimme tattoo parlours and tower blocks any day.'

Mum laughed. 'He could be a very silly man, your father. But he was a lovely one.' She frowned, looking mock-angry. 'Most of the time.' Then she sighed and said, 'Most of the time' again in a serious voice, this time meaning it.

Sometimes listening in is the only way for a kid to find out what is really happening in this world that adults make such a mess of. It's how I knew about Dad's financial screw-ups that made us go from OK off to poor as shit in the stopping of a heartbeat. It was a week after Dad's funeral. I was watching TV in the living room and Mum was on the phone to her friend Barbara in the kitchen. She shut the door between the kitchen and the living room because she knew I was only pretending to watch telly. I'm not sneaky, by the way, but sometimes it's got to be done. I tiptoed to the door and put my ear to the keyhole.

Dad had done something inexplicable and inexcusable that we will never get to the bottom of. Two things (apart from dying, obviously). He'd cashed in his life assurance policy. And he'd remortgaged our house in Camden Town against his business. Both without telling Mum. Which meant that after he died, and his company was found to be in serious debt, Mum and I were left up shit creek. The worst thing, Mum said to Barbara, was not being able to confront him with what he'd done and say, *Why?*

If only she and him could stand in the kitchen having a right old ding-dong about it for half an hour, it would be sorted. He'd have an explanation, she knew he would. He'd been stupid, but he hadn't been bad. There was no secret woman, or gambling addiction, or whatever. Or at least she was pretty sure there wasn't. Just one conversation, and the air would be cleared.

She said she didn't really mind giving up the one-and-a-half-million pound house in Gloucester Crescent,

25

or the five stays a year in the Caribbean, or the parties with rock stars and actors (at one party I was allowed at for ten minutes, Kevin Spacey gave me a keyring from a bar in Los Angeles but I lost it), or the New York shopping trips. She'd liked all that stuff but Dad was right: at heart she was just a country mouse and she would adjust. The only thing she really minded about was never being able to find out why he did what he did.

Well, bully for Mum, but what about me? Whoever asked me if I minded that God came along and took away my dad and my house and made me live in a shithole? In Gloucester Crescent I didn't just have a room, I had my own *floor*, for God's sake—Vern, Barry, and I played two-a-side footie in there with a half-sized ball. In the poncy old cottage there was hardly room to play pocket pool, if you know what I mean.

That first day in The Hollow, Mum said, 'Of course you must stay in touch with London. It's part of your life now and always will be. But you must make an effort to settle down here, too. You must make friends and not be snotty with people just because you think they're—what do you call them?'

'Manure munchers.'

'Charming. Where did you get that from? On second thoughts, I don't want to know.'

It's true, Bickleigh wasn't Outer Mongolia. It was worse. Corpse Central, I called it. There were extra-loud beeps on the pedestrian crossings so the dead people didn't get mown down by a manure-powered coffin driven at about three mph by another dead person. In the shops they took about three hours to walk four metres from the door to the counter. And because everyone was deaf they didn't hear that someone who wasn't dead (i.e. Mum and me and that was about it for about a hundred square miles) was behind them and trying to get past. If you didn't watch it they'd mow you down with the invalid scooters they drove on the pavements because they couldn't see where they were going: they were blind as well as deaf and dead.

If you were doing a lot of shopping in Bickleigh, it was best to take along something time-consuming to do—like memorizing every single statistic in the Official Arsenal Handbook—because people in shops took hours to serve you. First of all they were yakking on and on to the person in front of you about that day's prospects for the manure-eating contest or how Jemima got her leg chewed off by a combine harvester, then they were trying and failing to count out the right change because a) they couldn't see properly and b) they hadn't seen modern coins before, then they dropped the coins and had a heart attack trying to pick them up, then they had to have an afternoon nap, and then, when finally you got to the front of the queue and handed over your 20p for the sugar-rush you really needed five hours ago, they'd call you, 'Young sir.'

27

It was amazing to me that Camden High Street and Bickleigh High Street were both high streets existing in the same country at the same time. No giant Doc Marten boots or crashing silver planes stuck to the fronts of Bickleigh's buildings—make that Union Jacks on flagpoles and hanging baskets of flowers. No Rastas with dreads down to their bum-cracks, just corpses on day release from the mortuary, plus the occasional kid, crapped out in nylon with greasy centre-parted hair and bum fluff on his ears, toe-ending tin cans because that's as good as it gets in Manuresville. The Gobber would be regarded as cool if he relocated down here.

While I sat in the car waiting for Mum to buy her hand-crafted soup and weed cordial—I refused to get out and walk around in case they accidentally fitted me for a coffin—I would play a game. I imagined all the old gits I could see in front of me—shuffling along in their horrible pink anoraks that they probably bought from an advert in the back of *The Daily Telegraph*, with their white hair and flat feet, stopping to look at their shopping lists and having to put their specs on that hung round their necks, getting all misty-eyed about the Second World War, squelching their sweaty toes in their woolly socks and their footwear made by Clarks specially for geriatrics—I imagined them all gone. I pictured Bickleigh ethnically cleansed of dead people. For a few seconds, the wind and what it touched were the only moving things in Bickleigh. The Union Jack on a pole on the front of a big old house painted the same pink as those horrible anoraks. The St George's flag on top of the church. The banner advertising a Women's Fellowship lecture on 'The Wells of Old Wessex' in the village hall. Then Camden invaded.

All the nose jewellery and surfer chic and drug paraphernalia swept down the street like a tsunami, tearing down those old flags and putting up rainbow ones with PEACE written on them, turning the opticians into a Mexican fajita grill and sticking mannequins in bondage gear outside the estate agents and wax skull candles in the windows of Bickleigh Antiquarian Books.

I wish. Still, in those first few days in the country I did try really hard to be good and not call people manure munchers. Then: enter the Bozo, trailing bags of manure.

I was in the kitchen eating toast. We heard tyres crunching on the gravel in the drive. Mum looked at me and raised her eyebrows. A loud knock on the front door. Mum answered. Muffled words, a short, booming laugh, then the kitchen door was opening and a tall gangling man with polished-looking hair was invading the kitchen space, having to stoop. He smiled a putrid smile at me, as if a baby had just been sick on him.

'This is Mr Boland, love,' Mum said. 'He was a friend of your grandparents.'

'All right?' I said.

'Mercifully shipshape. And you may be?'

I didn't have to work at it, the name Bozo sprang to mind immediately.

'My galumphing son,' said Mum. 'Cup of tea?'

'Er . . . I'd better—' He looked at his watch. 'Well, ten minutes won't do any harm. Thank you.'

Mum cleared a space at the table so the Bozo could sit down. This involved putting away the butter and jam even though I hadn't finished with it. 'Oi,' I said, and Mum gave me her special bulgy-eyed frown.

'Before I forget, I've left something in the drive,' said the Bozo.

'Oh?' said Mum.

'Two bags of nature's finest. For your roses.'

'Sorry?' said Mum, who could be slow sometimes.

But I wasn't slow. I knew what it was straight away, and I got in there before the Bozo. 'Manure,' I shouted. 'Yes yes yes,' and I punched the air and did that Arsenal goal celebration with the pepper grinder.

The upshot of this car crash of an encounter was that Mum invited the Bozo and Mrs Bozo round for 'supper' the following Saturday. She got nervous, wondering what to cook. More nervous for a couple of manure munchers than when Eric Clapton came round to Gloucester Crescent, which was ridiculous. She didn't want to cook anything too fancy—like red snapper with garlic mash and purple sprouting broccoli hidden underneath it—in case it seemed too London, but she didn't think stew and dumplings was right either because they might think she thought they

30

were manure munchers (except she didn't say that, she said 'unsophisticated').

In the end she decided on lamb shanks, but in quite a London sauce that she got from the River Café cookbook. She asked if I would blend the soup for starters and chop up the celery and sun-dried tomatoes and find the capers for the lamb sauce.

'All I know is their names,' she said. 'Brian and Felicity Boland. I've no idea what they do. What are we going to talk about all evening?'

'Different sorts of manure,' I said. 'Manure to suit all occasions.'

Mum wagged her finger at me. 'Don't you dare.'

The couple were all dressed up. The Bozo was wearing a big shiny tie-thing covering his neck that Mum said afterwards was called a cravat. Felicity had on a flowery dress and a white shawl with tassels on draped round her shoulders. Mum had run out of time to change her clothes and was still wearing stripy dungarees. Oops. She showed them into the living room and asked me to ask them what they wanted to drink while she went into the kitchen to get some crisps and pistachio nuts. The Bozo said he'd have a small beer, because he was driving. Felicity wanted a white wine.

Just as I was going back into the kitchen to fetch the drinks the Bozo said, 'And which school do you attend?'

I said I didn't. I'd been at one in London, and I was going to a new one down here in the autumn but I couldn't remember its name.

31

The Bozo said, 'Our daughter Talullah is at Blunkers. Absolutely thriving there. Going great guns on the cello. You two should get acquainted.' He actually winked at me.

I said, 'Cool,' and went into the kitchen just as Mum came out with the bowls of crisps and nuts. While I got a can of beer out of the fridge I listened in to the conversation next door.

The Bozo said to Mum, 'Is your son down for Blunkers next term? He seemed a bit vague.'

Felicity said, 'You really couldn't make a better choice. Tally's so happy there.'

Mum said, 'No . . . um . . . He's just going to the local school in town.'

Felicity said, 'Ah.'

Tally! I almost gobbed in the Bozo's beer, but then that idea reminded me of the Gobber and I got depressed and tried to think of something else while I poured Felicity's wine. I thought of Dad's ashes, being blown by the wind on the Heath. If Dad was here now, in the kitchen with me, he'd be miming headbutting the bloke next door. Except he never would have been here. We were only here, living in this cottage and having this crappy couple round for dinner, because Dad wasn't here. That was the point. That was the deal, as Dad used to say.

Over the first course, which was the home-made soup that I'd mashed up in the blender, Mum asked the Bozo what he did for a job. He said, 'Plant hire.'

I looked at Mum and I had a bad feeling. She was suddenly looking really unhappy, holding her wine glass in mid-air as if her mechanism had wound down. She coughed and said, 'That's interesting. What, for weddings and things?'

The Bozo said, 'I beg your pardon?' Which is a crap thing to say.

Felicity said, 'Heavy plant. Steam rollers and grit blasters. Agricultural too. Brian is *the* supplier of combines and balers in the whole of the West Country, aren't you, Brian?'

'I have that distinction, I'm afraid. This soup's rather good. Is it a Delia?'

'Oh, how stupid of me,' said Mum. 'I was thinking of—I don't know what I was thinking of. I'm not really with it at the moment. The soup? No, it's . . . um—'

'It's just what we make,' I said. 'It's not from a recipe.'

'And do you work?' said Mum to Felicity.

'I find village life is taskmaster enough,' said Felicity. 'It keeps me terribly busy, I must say. The Women's Fellowship is under my aegis at the moment. You must come along, we have awfully good speakers. Are you gainfully employed yourself, Mrs McFall?'

'I will be, hopefully, from now on. My career's sort of been on hold for the last few years but it's time to dust it down and get on with it. Very much so.' Mum sighed and raised her eyebrows.

'And what is your career?' asked Felicity.

33

'I was a graphic designer. I'm hoping to set up here and work from home.'

'How nice.'

'Mum designed an album cover for Elvis Costello,' I said.

'I'll just get the main course,' said Mum. 'Collect the soup plates, will you, love?' she said to me.

Nobody talked for about ten minutes while we ate our lamb shanks. I was going to explain who Elvis Costello was, and what the album cover looked like that Mum designed, but I decided Mum wouldn't want me to.

All you could hear was the scraping of knives and forks. After a while it sounded deafening. Then Felicity said, 'This is nice, isn't it, Brian?'

The Bozo had his mouth full. He managed to say, 'Nnnn, very interesting.' When he'd swallowed properly he said to Mum, 'We were very sorry to hear of your father's death. So soon after your mother's.'

'Thank you,' said Mum. 'It's oddly comforting actually, that they should go so close together.' She laughed. 'It's certainly been a hell of a year.'

The Bozo held his knife and fork in mid-air and had his head on one side. He looked as if he was about to burst into tears. 'Yes. We understand your life has taken an even more tragic turn in recent times. Your husband also. Awfully bad luck.'

'Yes, we're terribly sorry for your loss,' said Felicity.

'Thank you, that's kind. Yes, it's been very hard. Still, we're down here now and we're starting afresh, aren't we, love?' I nodded. 'Actually, it's a home-coming of sorts for me. You probably don't know, because there are few people left in the village who remember me now, but I was actually brought up here.'

'Oh,' said Felicity, and did a big nod.

'Yes, I know this, actually,' said the Bozo. He grinned and looked relieved that he didn't have to pretend he was sensitive any more. 'I remember you. Clare Groves. Good little gymnast. Plaits, if I remember rightly.' He wiggled his fingers either side of his head. 'I'm the Brian who lived in Bickleigh. Remember that derelict old place Hedge End Hall, that we tried to break into as kids? That's where we are now. We did the place up and developed it as a commercial site. We have a portfolio of agricultural interests operating from the one base.'

Mum was so surprised she forgot where she was and went all London. 'Hullo?' she said, really loudly, speaking like a policeman with learning difficulties.


After they'd gone, Mum hit the red wine and got drunk. She was sitting in Grandma's armchair. She'd kicked off her sandals and had her legs curled up on the seat. 'I mean, I can't believe it,' she kept saying. 'That stupid, stupid man. That complete anal retentive tosspot. He's already been here once and he still doesn't mention that he knows me. It takes him two bloody hours! What's that all about? I can't believe

35

I said that about plant hire, though. I was thinking of, I don't know, hiring out palm trees in tubs for wedding marquees, or something like that. I mean, that's not so stupid is it? Oh, I'm sorry, love. You really catch the brunt of it, don't you?'

'Can I have some wine?' I said.

'Get a glass,' she said. 'Fill it with a bit of water first.' When I'd come back with the glass she poured me a slosh and said, 'I don't know, love. It's like another planet to me now, the village. It's weird because when I'm in London I don't feel I belong there, and I come down here, to where I grew up, and it's like bloody Outer Mongolia. Oh God!' She took an extra-big glug of wine, then laughed so much she had to spit half of it back. 'I mean, talk about dysfunctional.'

'He's a complete bozo,' I said. 'Brian the Bozo. And Felicity Flapdoodle.'

Mum giggled, then shuddered. 'Hey, guess what? I remember him now. He made a pass at me once at a Young Farmers' dance. Can you believe it? Aggghhh!'

The morning after the Bozos had been for dinner, I went down to the kitchen in my Arsenal dressing gown and Mum put a bacon butty in front of me. I opened up the butty, gave it a good dollop of Daddy's brown sauce, and took a mouthful. 'Hey, this picture of a daddy on the sauce bottle looks like Brian the Bozo,' I said.

'Please,' said Mum. 'Don't remind me.' She was drinking coffee, strong and black, which she'd poured from a large cafetière. 'I shouldn't have finished off that red wine. I've got Mrs Plunkett-Strawberry coming round this morning to tell me about Neighbourhood Watch.'

I laughed. 'Plunkett-Strawberry? You're joking.'

'Well, something like that. Double-barrelled anyway. Look, love, I've been thinking and I really think I've been so self-centred and wrapped up in my own problems in the last few weeks and I want to make it up to you, and I'd like to buy you a really good mountain bike, if you'd like one. I've got a bit of money set aside. What do you think? You could go exploring. The roads are extremely safe round here. You can get away from me for a few hours every day. That'll be really nice won't it?'

I nodded and shrugged. How boring was that? I was thinking. But we were both of us wrong. The roads of Manuresville weren't safe and boring. They were dangerous.

# Chapter 3

In London we had what Vern called a manor. It was triangular shaped, with Hampstead Heath (where the school was) at the apex and Camden Town and Chalk Farm tubes at its base points. This is where we hung out, on the buses and pavements and in the shops, laughing at divs and doing a bit of light shoplifting, nothing industrial.

Now my manor was a country lane, and a bit of main road, and—as I was about to discover—a shit-hole of a shop. First thing I did on the mountain bike (which was the second cheapest in the bike shop in Basingstoke, but I didn't say anything) was check out this new manor. From the gate of the cottage, I turned into the lane and freewheeled for a mile or more, on about the same incline as from Kentish to Camden Towns, between high hedges and tall trees, past a pond with yellow flowers growing round its edge, dodging horseshit on the road and trying to run over cig packets, overtaken by a Land Rover pulling a horsebox, and a Toytown cop car who gave me a toot, probably for not wearing a tweed cap. The sunlight came side-ways, in blinding speckles, through the hedges and

38

trees and as the wind rushed in my ears I felt myself tipping down a green chute.

I remembered us driving up this lane in the BMW with the serious sound system, in another lifetime that was only a year ago. Dad bipped his horn at every bend in case a car was coming the other way. Mum wanted him to wind the windows down, let the country air in, but Dad preferred keeping the car sealed so the air con worked. This is the kind of thing they argued about but it was only mock arguing. Mum and Dad really loved each other, is what I mean.

The hedges and trees stopped, the road flattened out, and I had to brake to stop my momentum carrying me across a busy road. Resting on the handlebars I watched the traffic for a bit. Sometimes I hated being a kid, without the money to do what you liked, like jump in a car and disappear.

I turned my bike right, onto the wide grass verge of the main road. Half a mile along was the shop, a red-brick building with a green awning on the front advertising a crap lager that only complete divs drink. Underneath the awning were stacked empty orange plastic crates. On the front of the shop it said 'One-Stop Shop'. Someone had changed the 'Shop' to 'Poop' with a spraycan (major comedians inhabited the neighbourhood, obviously).

My idea was to stock up with cans and cereal bars, see what DVDs there were (none, as it turned out;

probably still getting to grips with smoke signals) and generally suss the place out seeing as it was the only shop and hang-out joint for miles around. A bell rang on the door when I opened it, then silence until I started coughing. Getting asphyxiated wasn't part of the plan. Dude, that smell was serious.

The shop stank of old blokes and farts and something even more nasty that I couldn't put my finger on at first. It wasn't just the smell that was unpleasant. The apples were so old they'd gone yellow and wrinkled. The wrappers on the chocolate bars were shrivelled and bleached from lying so long in the sun that blazed through the window. There was a crap model aeroplane with an elastic-band propeller for sale that looked about thirty years old. But the worst thing was the deli counter which was just a bunch of old ice-cream tubs with different coloured gunky stuff in them that was going dry at the edges and had flies crawling on it. Rats would think twice, as Dad once said about a lasagne we had in Scotland.

There was a passageway through to the back, divided halfway along by a curtain of plastic coloured strips. After a minute of me poking about and trying to keep my breakfast down, a pair of tartan slippers appeared below the curtain, and a belly in a cardigan and a hairy head pushed through the strips. It was my first sighting of the Smelly Man.

His eyes were watery, like egg whites that haven't been cooked properly, his skin was grey, his head hair was grey-yellow like the air in a pub, and his beard was an industrial-strength pan scrubber stuck on his chin. As he shuffled forward he put his hands on the counter for balance. His fingernails were black and there were scabs and sores across his knuckles, with plasters hiding the leaky ones. 'Now then,' he said. When he spoke, a clanking noise started deep inside his chest that sounded like someone pulling a toilet chain in a stately home. 'What can I do you for, young man?'

As well as the smell of the shop, the SM had his own, unique fragrance. It was made up of sixty fags a day, and booze, and really old, too-tight, nylon underpants, but there was something else in there that was disgustingly familiar. I looked away, trying not to sick up the bacon and orange juice that was queuing in my throat and wondering where I'd smelt that smell before. Then I remembered.

Dad in hospital, lying opposite an old bloke who looked like Death. This old bloke had loads of tubes attached, including below decks, and sometimes when Mum and I were there the old bloke would throw off his bedcothes and lie there naked looking like a supermarket chicken that someone is doing experiments on.

Then the nurse would come in and cover him up but always his feet stuck out of the end of the bedclothes, pointing towards Dad's bed. And his toes had stuff between them that looked like old cream cheese, that used to be white but had gone yellow at the edges (what cream cheese would look like if the Smelly Man stocked it in his so-called deli). But the thing about this toe cheese was, it didn't just look extremely unpleasant. Occasionally I would get a whiff, as I sat on that hard chair trying to pretend to Dad that my life and his were more or less normal, and when that whiff reached my nostrils it was a million days in hell all concentrated into a split second. And now I knew how to describe the smell. It was the smell of the Smelly Man.

'Got any chorizo sausage?' I managed to say.

'(*Cough*) What's chorizo (*wheeze*)?' said the SM.

'It's OK,' I said, backing away. 'What about ciabatta bread?'

'Are you being funny?' he said, and pulled a packet of snouts out of his cardigan pocket.

'No, it's OK. Cheers. See you later.'

I cycled like a maniac after I got out of that shop—cut back along the grass verge of the main road and took a left up the hill towards the cottage. It was then, with the smell of the Smelly Man still clinging to my nostrils, that I first saw the boy who tried to steal my life.

As I turned off the main road it started to rain, big fat splats cracking like eggs on the dusty lane. Through the overhanging branches, the sky had turned a bruised colour, the colour of the damsons Mum was pretending to be excited about in the back garden. Soon the rain was whooshing down as strong as stones, flattening the greenery on the verges of the lane, pummelling the backs

42

of my hands on the handlebars. I hopped the bike off the tarmac and skidded up a bank to the trunk of the nearest roadside tree, vaulted off the saddle, and flattened myself against the scaly, surprisingly warm bark.

The violent downpour had already turned one side of the lane into a gurgling stream but where I stood, tucked under an angle of the trunk, was almost completely dry. There I stayed, my arms spread out against the trunk, my cheek nudging against the nobbles of bark, my eyes gazing on the sheeting, rumbling rain, shivering a bit with the sudden cold. And, then, through the rain, a figure walked.

More hovered than walked, that's how it looked. His feet made no sound, or at least the rain was so loud now that it drowned out all lesser sounds. And there was no sense that the figure—a boy, I saw now, a kid maybe my age—knew it was raining. Because everybody reacts to weather. If it's cold you hunch your body up, if it's hot you open yourself to the sun, you turn your face up like a flower in the morning. And if it starts raining torrentially, you keep your head down and run for shelter. But this kid wasn't running, or even walking quickly, and he wasn't keeping his head down.

He was walking quite slowly down the lane in the direction of the main road, looking about him a bit as he went, as if he was the only person in a school corridor and he was late for a lesson but didn't care that he was late because it was a lesson he always found boring. Which made him look kind of cool even though, from what I could make out through the rain, he was thin and gangly, with big feet, wore cheapo trainers and a crap pair of too-tight shorts with zips, and had a regulation bumpkin mong centre parting.

Closer and closer he got. Surely he would see me now, or if not me then my bike? Flattened there against the tree, I braced myself for the moment he spotted me and cried out in surprise. But he never did see me. Something else happened though. It was like a burst of white noise in my head, as if my mind was suddenly a radio receiver and a signal had zapped into it. A signal I couldn't decipher. It sounds stupid, but for that split second I wondered if the kid was some sort of visitor, trying to communicate in a way that was beyond human scope. And, of course, as it panned out, he was a visitor in a way, but not in the way that I ever could have imagined then.

Weirded out, I shook my head to free it of the electric chaos, then started to say something, to offer to share my shelter with him: 'Hey—' But the rain took my voice and drowned it in the gurgle of rainwater on tarmac, the smack of rainwater on leaves, and the kid carried on walking, past the tree, past my bike slewed across the muddy bank, not looking, not hearing, not caring, and disappeared round the corner.

Five minutes later the rain eased as quickly as it had started. I pulled up my bike from the sodden bank and wiped the saddle. I was about to resume my journey back to the cottage when the sun came out, fanning through the branches, turning the rainwater to wisps of steam on the lane, and I changed my mind, turning the bike round and pushing off downhill instead. Each bend I went round, I expected to see the kid trundling along at the side of the lane in his spooky, manure-muncherish way. But he wasn't there. I reached the main road, looked left and right. Nothing. I shrugged, assuming he must have taken a short cut through the woods to wherever he was going, and, for the moment, I forgot about the weird kid who appeared through the rain and vanished into it again.

I had no idea where I was going, I just followed my front tyre: turned right towards the Smelly Man's shop, then took the first left before the shop and headed up the incline of a narrow lane hemmed in by tall hedgerows. At the top of the hill was an open plateau of yellow crops. The lane cut through the yellow field and swept down into a wide valley of green fields and hedges stretching many kilometres to a horizon of jagged trees that looked like teeth. This sudden, distant view made me catch my breath. I inhaled deeply, to get my breath back and to clear any toe cheese pong that the rain hadn't managed to wash away. I laughed, remembering the Smelly Man. It was a good story, I couldn't wait to tell—to tell who? I didn't know anyone I could tell, apart from Mum, and she would say I was being unfair and cruel (which is what she did say).

Leaning on the handlebars, I gazed on the view. The world seemed happy and relieved after the rain. Grasshoppers made a sound like microscopic violins in the verges. Birds sang and swooped in the trees and air. High up, a plane was crossing the now-clear sky. My eyes picked it up and followed it well before the noise of its engines leaked down through the blue. And from the foot of the valley in front of me came a muffled squawking that sounded like hundreds of chickens.

My eyes followed the chicken sound. At the bottom of the hill was a sizeable development containing a large, old stone house with tall chimneys, numerous outbuildings and metal barns, and huge, dark trees with spreading branches, all enclosed by a security fence that glinted in the sunlight.

I pushed my bike to the start of the descent into the valley. I would never have admitted it to Vern or Barry, or even to my mum, but standing there in the sunlight, with all these noises playing soothingly in the background, and the steam rising off the roads, which really did look strange and magical, I felt a blip of happiness, the first I had felt for a long time, followed by an irresistible impulse: to ride down into the valley as fast as I could.

Contouring my body against the crossbar, I pedalled like crazy. My legs felt strong, more like machine parts, like well-oiled bits of bike, than blood and bone and muscle. The thick tyres made a fast, snaky sound on the wet road, kicking up a fine mist that covered me like a garden sprinkler. I pushed on, faster and faster, round the blind bends.

It was a single track road, with passing places every so often. There was no point keeping in to the left-hand side, I told myself. All of the road belonged to me. But just in case a car, or tractor, or other form of transport favoured by manure munchers should whip round a corner, and seeing as I didn't have a bell or horn, and because I just fancied clearing my lungs out anyway, I yelled out as I went, 'What do we want? Tattoo parlours and kebab houses! When do we want 'em? Now!' And so I went with it, with the wind whistling across my helmet, the insects spattering in my eyes and on my lips, with the mist soaking my legs, trusting to the wolf-spirit. Mistake!

As the road began to flatten out, the security fence appeared on the left-hand side. I was still yelling when I went round the last bend. I didn't stand a chance. The driver was in the process of turning out of the driveway at the end of the row of trees and the lorry was stranded right across the road. I just had time to raise my hands instinctively from the handlebars. They caught the side of the lorry and the impact knocked me backwards on to the road, while the bike got jammed under the truck (and was completely bollocksed).

The words 'kebab shops' hung in the air. Amazingly I wasn't hurt, except for scraped hands which stung like hell. I lay there facing a smooth grass bank. Planted in it was a wooden sign with black letters burnt into it. I had to lift my head so I could read the sign. It said: Hedge End Hall Farm Products. Then the driver was clambering down from his cab and yelling, and another man was running out of the driveway behind the lorry, also yelling.

The bloke from the driveway got to me first. It was Brian the Bozo.

Mum went ballistic. Not with me but with life. She had thought it was impossible to come to harm, down here in wonderful Manure Land. She got the incident out of proportion and had a crying fit. I said it wasn't a big deal, I'd just run into a lorry, that's all. It could have happened anywhere. And then she screamed at me, which was unusual.

'That's the point,' she said. 'It could happen anywhere. The truth is, nowhere's safe. I came down here to get us out of harm's way. But it's not possible.' And then she squeezed me almost to death.

I was bloody annoyed about it too: not because of the scraped knuckles and torn T-shirt—very minor shit—but because it gave Brian the Bozo a reason to worm his way into Mum's life. After the lorry incident bloody Brian wouldn't keep away from The Hollow. First of all he took me home in his Land Rover Discovery with my bent bike in the back, and stood in our kitchen watching and smiling while Mum wiped the scrapes on my hands with TCP and put plasters on them (as soon as he'd left she had the crying fit). Then he insisted on buying me a new mountain bike, seeing as his lorry had been blocking the road and it was all his fault (and seeing as it was a good excuse to come round and see Mum again. It was a half-decent bike though, I'll give him that). Then, when he just happened to be passing, he called in to say he thought it would be a good idea to bring his daughter Tally round to play, seeing as I hadn't had time to make any friends yet. To play! Tally!

We were standing in the kitchen. Mum had offered the Bozo coffee and he had accepted, which pissed me off. Mum was leaning back against the work surface with a robot grin on her face. I suddenly pictured the strange kid walking through the rain. A memory of white noise passed from ear to ear through my brain, and before I knew what I was saying I burst out with: 'But I have got a friend.'

'Oh. Have you, dear?' Mum said, looking a bit confused. I bulged out my eyes for a split-second to tell her I was pretending, but I wasn't pretending, not really. The kid was already humming in my head and I hadn't even met him yet. Still, she played along. 'Oh, of course,' she said. 'I'd forgotten about him. What's his name again?'

'I'll tell you later,' I said. 'I'm off to meet him now.' And I was out of The Hollow and down the road faster than you can say Tally the Toffee-Nosed Tart, with Mum shouting after me, 'Don't forget your knee and elbow protectors,' which is what she'd bought me after the lorry incident but I never wore them, I just stashed them in my backpack.

Enter, obligingly, the kid himself, twiddling me like a dial, tuning me in—not that I remotely realized that at the time. It happened a couple of days after Brian had mentioned bringing Tally round. It was raining again. The wind was bending the trees and roaring in the branches. I was lying on my bed listening to some punkabilly on my cheapo sound system and not thinking of the kid at all—or even, surprisingly, of my Dad—but picturing Camden Lock, one and three quarter hours and a million miles away, when I heard the crunch of tyres in the drive. I looked out and saw the Bozo and the blonde bonce and thick-rimmed swot-specs of his darling daughter next to him in the front seat of the bozomobile. There they sat, a boxed set of dorks, and I knew I had to escape, even if a near-hurricane was blowing.

The timing had to be right. I went out of the french windows at the end of the cottage below my bedroom, and waited there till I heard Mum calling my name, which meant the Bozos were now inside the cottage. Then I ran round the back of the house, keeping below the level of the windows, to the garage. I was soaked by the time I reached my bike but I didn't care. I ran it down the drive, jumped on and escaped into a Bozo-free zone.

I'd taken the mudguards off my new bike because mudguards make a bike look crap, which meant I didn't just get soaked from the rain, I got all this mud from the road splashing me front and back. But it didn't matter. In fact it was brilliant. Having already seen the kid walking through the rain as if it didn't exist, I knew that getting soaked, as long as it's in the summer and therefore basically warm, is one of the best things you can do. Because when you get soaked, NOTHING MATTERS somehow. So there I was, bombing down the hill towards the main road with not much of an idea of where I was going, but feeling very cool and free, and I whizzed past a boy walking along the side of the road.

What I did next is called a Statue of Liberty. Barry Lunc's brother showed me how, he once did it on the bridge at Camden Lock and terrified a Jap tourist. I slammed on the front brake, slewed the back wheel round with my arse, hopped off on the right side of the bike, locked on the rear brake, jumped on the back tyre, hopped us both, the bike and me, into balance, punched my left fist up through the rain (so I looked like the famous statue, see?), and shouted in the boy's face, 'Hey, respect it. Respect that rain. You get my meaning?' I said it in a London voice, of course, the only way to say it.

It was only then, balanced on the back wheel with that marf-fulla London street talk still echoing through the wind and rain, that I realized this boy was the kid I'd seen before. The rain had flattened his hair down his cheeks so it looked as if someone had tipped a skip of cooking oil on the top of his head. His mouth hung open with the shock of a face full of me. I imagined seeing him on the towpath when I was with Vern. We'd nudge each other and giggle. Now that I could see him more clearly, the whole effect of him seemed wrong. His hair was long but it didn't looked planned, it had just grown like a weed—and the centre parting was vintage mong. The T-shirt and shorts were the opposite of surf-baggy, which was the only way to look, the way we looked in Camden. And the legs and feet! Matchsticks stuck in jumbo sausage rolls. And when he opened his mouth, boring shit came out in a full-on bumpkin accent: 'It's still raining less than it used to,' he said. 'The water table's dropped quite a bit round here in the last few years.'

I didn't know what he meant, which made me feel stupid, especially after the Statue of Liberty misjudgement. I nodded and jumped off the bike. 'What you doing, anyway?' I said. No London, just normal.

And now, standing face to face with him, I spotted something else. How could I have missed it first time round? He had no earlobes, or at least he had no dangle in them. He was a slimehead like me. Like Mum and like my grandpa and, who knows, probably a whole cemetery full of my slimehead ancestors.

But if he noticed this unusual physical feature that we had in common, he didn't show it. He just shrugged and stared at me. A drop of rainwater was growing bigger on the end of his nose but he didn't brush it off or shake his head to dislodge it.

I said, 'D'you live round here?'

'Not far away. You?' He continued to stare.

'Just back there.' I jerked my thumb over my shoulder. Still the kid didn't move, or show any expression.

Maybe he was autistic. It suddenly seemed ridiculous, standing here wasting my time with this loser. He wasn't a visitor from outer space, he was just a div. The thought made me depressed. This is probably what all the kids were like round here. No chance of making friends, unless of course I chose to have the op—the personality and humour bypass—and became one of them. 'Anyway . . . ' I said, and started to step round the kid, intending to put several kilometres between me and him as quickly as possible.

Maybe it was just a coincidence but he moved the same way at the same time, and the effect was to block me. I looked down at his huge clumsy feet, trying to tell him with my eyes that he was invading my space and I wanted to get on.

He didn't take the hint. Instead he said, 'What's your name, anyway?'

I sighed, because I'm not exactly proud of the name, and said, 'Mungo.'

The effect on the kid was amazing, as if a corpse had been injected with Tourette's Syndrome. He lifted his hands and trembled them like a comical preacher-man, he wobbled his head, gave several short, hard little nods, then tilted his head back and mouthed, 'Yes!' at the rainy sky.

Nutter or what? I was thinking. I said, 'You all right?' and squeezed the handlebars of my bike, wanting more than ever to vamoose.

He became quiet and still again, and resumed the staring. And I had a peculiar sensation, a kind of animal fear. If I'd been a wolf I'd have been backing off the kid and growling.

'I'm fine,' said the kid. And then he gave a loud laugh.

'What's so funny?'

'You really want to know?'

I shrugged, feeling somehow humiliated as well as frightened.

'I'm called Mungo too,' said the kid.

# Chapter 4

It was my turn to stare. 'Oh right,' I said after a pause. I was trying to keep calm, think it through. A weird guy and a weird coincidence, that was all. I wanted more than ever to disappear, but now felt obliged to have the conversation. 'I was named after my great-grandfather,' I said.

'Me too,' said Mungo.

'He was Scottish.'

'So was mine.'

Now we both stared. 'No shit,' I said.

We stood in silence for a few more seconds, then Mungo said, 'Did your great-grandfather invent radar?'

'Not that I know of,' I said.

Mungo narrowed his eyes as if he didn't believe me. 'Are you sure?'

No, I wasn't bloody sure! I didn't know anything about my Scottish great-grandfather beyond the fact that he had a stupid name and died before I was born. He could have been world haggis-eating champion for all I knew. But I was getting worried now. 'Course I'm sure,' I said.

But Mungo wouldn't let it go. 'What about a book?' he said. 'Did he write a book?'

'What about?'

'About—' Mungo hesitated and looked away. 'Just about things. Scientific things.'

'Nah. Definitely not,' I said.

Mungo did his preacherman act with his hands again. 'Forget it,' he said. 'Must be a coincidence. They happen more than people realize.' Now he rubbed his hands together and changed the subject. 'I know somewhere that's dry where we can build a fire and get warm. Shall we—?' He didn't finish the sentence.

I hesitated. Those split-seconds when events can go one way or another. 'I dunno,' I said, 'I'm just—'

'May as well,' he said. And the way he was looking—imploring—I was suddenly flattered that he wanted my company. Which is what happens if you stay on your tod for long enough in the people-free wastes of Manuresville.

'All right, just for a bit then,' I said. 'Which way?'

He pointed down the lane towards the main road and I indicated that he should hop on the back of the bike.

The main road was more like a shallow sea. Headlights on at 11a.m., bumpers making bow waves through the rain. As we watched the cars I turned my head and said over my shoulder, 'Do people call you Mong sometimes?'

Mungo didn't answer the question. Instead he said, 'You have attached earlobes like me.'

I said, 'We're both slimeheads, you mean.'

He just smiled and dismounted from my bike. 'Let's go to the shop first,' he said. 'It's just along here. I need to buy matches.'

'I'll wait outside,' I said. 'You could catch a killer disease in there.'

'Why?' said Mungo.

'Have you seen his hands? Touch those by accident and you'll pick up something terminal, I reckon.'

'Because he's queer?'

'What you on about?' I said. Typical. You meet a manure muncher in the middle of nowhere and you're so desperate to talk to a non-corpse you kid yourself he's OK. A bit weird but basically sound. But he ain't OK, he's a homophobic bigot who probably also thinks that stoning adulterers is reasonable social policy. And he assumes I'm a bigot too. 'No!' I said. 'I meant, because his hands look as if they've got some horrible disease. Anyway the word's gay. But the Smelly Man isn't gay, that I've noticed.'

'Well, he's not smelly that I've noticed,' said Mungo. 'Come on.'

And that's when I discovered that the Smelly Man's shop was no more. The brick shell of it was the same, but the facade and the interior had been changed into a bright new emporium of the sort you might find in Hampstead, frequented by actors wearing long coloured scarves and buying olives. Large windows with strings of garlic and leafy branches hanging up in them instead of plastic crates and dead wasps. New sign in loopy lettering that said 'Gavin's Deli' instead of 'One-Stop Shop/Poop'.

Hurray! The Smelly Man had finally expired in his own whiff and a new bloke had taken the shop over, hopefully from London.

I waited outside while Mungo went in to buy matches. When he came out I said, 'So where is this place we're going to?'

'The Happy Valley? It's not far at all now.'

I cycled us back down the main road until Mungo tapped me on the shoulder to tell me we should take a right turn. I managed about twenty metres up a hill between tall hedgerows before the weight of my passenger ground us to a halt. We dismounted and walked to the top of the hill. On the way he said, 'So where exactly do you live?'

'Cottage called The Hollow.' I pulled a face. 'Boring. What about you?'

He pointed vaguely to the left. 'D'you know the road to Bickleigh? Just off of that. It's got pineapples on the gateposts.'

'But I'm from London,' I said. 'We just moved.' My eyes watered a bit when I said London because I suddenly felt sentimental for the old place. London was the greatest city on earth and I was part of it. Still part of it, whatever anybody said.

'London?' Mungo laughed disbelievingly. ''Spect you're glad to be out of it, aren't you?'

I wanted to call him Mong then. He hadn't just insulted me, he'd insulted my dad. What was left of my dad that was blowing around on Hampstead Heath. Why was I even talking to such a kid, who was also a homophobic bigot, let alone giving him rides on my bike? Because this was a crap place where no one interesting lived and you ended up talking to mongs because otherwise you'd have to talk to trees.

When I didn't reply, Mungo said, 'So what does your dad do?'

'Record producer.'

'Wow. Is he famous?'

I'm sorry, Dad, I lied about you, and it wasn't to protect you, either, it was to protect me. Somehow I didn't want this weird kid that I'd only just met knowing about your current status of being dead. Something told me he might use it against me—but not telling him was a mistake, as it panned out.

'In his own circles, yeah,' I said. 'He knows famous people.'

'Like who?'

'Eric Clapton? Kevin Spacey?'

Mungo shrugged.

'What, you haven't heard of them?' I said. I couldn't believe it. 'Have you heard of Elvis Presley?'

'Course I have,' said Mungo. 'Have you heard of Erwin Schroedinger?'

'Who's he?'

'He was a magician. Kind of.' Mungo paused, then said, 'Is your dad strict?'

I laughed. 'Nah. He's not really like a dad. More like a mate. He lets me drink beer and stuff. He's just cool really.'

It was a lovely feeling, talking about Dad as if he was still alive. And afterwards, when I thought about it, it would be a very sad feeling.

'Does he love your mum?'

The question took me by surprise. 'Dunno,' I said, and then felt annoyed with myself, because I knew the real answer was: yeah, loads.

'Does he have rows with her though?' asked Mungo.

'Only pretend ones, most of the time. What is this? Guantanamo Bay?'

'Do they, you know—'

'What?'

'You know, still do it.'

'Bloody hell,' I said, 'are you a perv or what?' Mungo's questioning was creepy. 'Do yours?' I said.

'You must be joking,' Mungo said. And when he suddenly accelerated, striding on ahead to the top of the hill, I had an idea he did it so I couldn't see his face.

Dragging my bike along with me, I caught up with him at the top and recognized where I was. Facing us was the plain of fields and hedges stretching to a horizon of jagged trees. No glinting sunlight this time, no happy grasshoppers sounding off in the hedgerows, just the gusting rain moving the fields around and below us in lazy liquid swirls. But this was surely the place I'd reached on my bike, before zooming off downhill to collide with the lorry.

But the view was sort of different. Down near the foot of the hill there had been a security fence surrounding a big old house and farm buildings, the place where I ran into the truck: Hedge End Hall Farm, home of the Bozos, Brian, Felicity, and Tally. But now, as I looked, there was no fence here, and though there was a similar looking house, with tall chimneys, there were no outbuildings or barns. Instead the house was surrounded, and practically swallowed, by dark woodland that suggested a deep gash of land far below the tree line. Where we were now standing was like the hill I'd reached before, but it wasn't the same one.

Mungo pointed down at the gash of trees and the tall chimneys. 'That's it,' he said, 'Happy Valley and Happy Valley House,' and set off ahead of me again, his tentacle legs taking long impatient strides down the hill. I watched his shoulderblades pumping like phantom wings through his rain-sodden T-shirt, then launched myself onto my bike and freewheeled to catch him up.

The weather was weeping across the valley, the rain gusting in mesmerizing swirls like a screen saver. But even as I watched, dropping down the hill, the weather—and the view—changed. A sudden flash of lightning—weirdly, there was no thunder—came out of nowhere.

61

I almost fell off the saddle with the shock of it, and when I looked up a rip of blue had appeared in the dark clouds. The wind blew the rip bigger and bigger until all of a sudden the sun burst through like in an advert for butter or washing powder, flooding the valley in a golden yell of happiness. The cornfields turned into rippling Brazilian football jerseys, birds sang and, when I lifted a hand from the handlebar to check, I discovered it had stopped raining. 'Hey!' I said peering ahead to where I thought Mungo was.

But Mungo had dissolved into the soft summer air.

When I got back to the cottage the bozomobile had gone from the driveway. Mum said, 'Where've you been, for God's sake? Didn't you have your phone with you? I've been trying to call you.'

I said, 'It doesn't pick up round here,' which was true. 'I've been with . . . ' Who had I been with? Had I been with anyone, or was I now so sad that I was inventing imaginary friends like a dysfunctional three year old? Already it seemed a little bit unreal: the name, the earlobes, all the stuff about my great-grandfather, the spooky way he'd disappeared. In any case, I certainly couldn't call him Mungo, Mum'd think I really was mad. ' . . . Steve,' I said.

'Who's Steve?'

'I told you. The friend I told you about.' Mum narrowed her eyes and wrinkled her nose. She was doing what she called Smelling a Rat. 'You know. I mentioned him when the Bozo was here before. He's called Steve and I've met him a couple of times and we'd arranged to meet.'

'In the torrential rain? And Mr Boland's name is Brian, by the way.'

'Yeah. Rain's not a big deal. Rain's cool. Everyone thinks they have to shelter from it but they don't. You should try just standing in it and getting really soaked. It feels good.'

'Did your dad tell you that?'

'No way. What's Dad got to do with it?'

'You need a hot bath. You'll catch a chill. Where does he live then, this Steve?'

'I don't know.'

'You don't know?'

I remembered about the pineapples. 'Hang on. He said near Bickleigh or something.'

'It was very rude of you, Mungo.' She only used my full name like that when she was angry. 'It made it really awkward with Brian and Talullah. I had to lie for you. When you didn't come down after I'd called you, I had to pretend I'd forgotten you were going out. That's not fair, Mungo.'

I said, 'Brian and Talullah Boland. Ooooo!'

Mum put her hands on her hips. 'So where have you been?'

'I told you. With Steve. And I don't give a monkey's whether you believe me or not because it's true. Oh yeah, and Tally can piss off too cos no way am

63

I hanging out with a posh manure muncher like that.'

Mum went ominously quiet. She said, 'I'm just going to say one thing. I don't like deviousness. Deviousness is creeping in and I won't have it. And I won't have swearing in this house. Do you understand, Mungo?'

I said, 'That's two things.'

'Mungo!!' Afterwards, in the silence, I could hear grandad's clock ticking in the living room.

'Yeah?'

'I don't want to be around you at the moment. Have your bath. Then go to your room.'

Before my bath I tiptoed into Mum's room. I had to be really careful because the house was so old it creaked. I got down on the floor and peered under Mum's bed. After Dad died, there was one thing of his that Mum kept, or rather two things: his leopardskin creepers. Everything else of his disappeared in binbags when I was at school one day, including the belt that Keith Richards wore on a Rolling Stones world tour in the 1980s (I didn't talk to her for a week after that took a walk). But the creepers she put under her bed. Not just under, so you could get them out easily, but right in the middle so you had to lie flat on the floor and stretch your arm out, and even then you needed something in your hand like a coathanger to reach them. She didn't know that I knew she kept them under her bed. And now I was checking that they were still there, that they had made the journey safely from Camden Town to Manuresville.

They were there all right, right in the middle. I hoiked out the nearest, the left one, with the coathanger I'd brought and pressed the shoe to my nose as if it was an oxygen mask. I breathed in deeply, hoovering up the Dad smell, then I held the shoe to my ear and turned it into a telephone. 'Hey, Dad,' I said. 'Help me out here. What the hell's going on?'

That evening Mum made pheasant, which I wasn't into because it had been shot by posh manure munchers and still had bullets in it. I picked out the bits of lead and piled them on the side of the plate.

Mum watched me for a bit then sighed and said, 'Are you actually going to eat any of that or are you just going to excavate it? You're determined to give me a hard time today, aren't you?'

I said, 'Why did you call me Mungo? I hate it. It's a crap name.'

'You know very well why. It was my grandfather's name.'

'Yeah, but why couldn't it have been my second name, the one you never use. Then I could have been just plain Mark or Dave.'

'Then it wouldn't work, would it? The whole point was to keep his memory alive. You should be proud.

He was a special man. Ahead of his time. The people who laughed at him were pygmies compared to him.'

'Why did they laugh at him?'

'Because he wasn't afraid to think difficult thoughts and say difficult things. Now at least eat the vegetables.'

'Was he a slimehead like us?'

'Don't call it that, love. We can't all be alike. Anyway, we have perfectly normal ears and so did my grandfather.'

'So he was a slimehead then. Did he invent radar?'

Mum froze, with her knife and fork in mid-air. 'He always claimed to have done, yes. And I have always believed that he did, even if he never got the credit. How did you know about that?'

I managed to stay dead casual and say, 'Er . . . I think Dad told me once.'

I waited a couple of minutes, doing my best to actually eat the pheasant rather than just re-arrange it, then I said, 'So did this guy write a book too?'

Mum put her knife and fork down and stared at me with her smelling-a-rat face. 'As a matter of fact he did,' she said. 'How much do you know?'

'I don't know anything,' I said, pretending it was no big deal. 'I'm just making conversation.'

'When did your father tell you this?'

'Oh, I dunno, on one of our walks down here, I think, when Dad wanted to escape from Gran's wittering. Can you have brown sauce on pheasant?'

Mum ignored the question and said, 'Your grandpa

had a copy of the book, you know. He was in two minds whether to keep it but I think he threw it out eventually. Along with some other stuff. His father's pipe-rack, things like that. Bad memories. I'll tell you all about it one day, when I'm more up for it.'

'Whatever,' I said, as if I was hardly listening. But inside my chest it felt as if my heart was doing double beats.

All night they gnawed away at my brain, giving me no sleep: the tricks Mungo had played. The stuff about my great-grandfather's name and the book he had written, then the disappearing act. This must be what people did down here because there was nothing else to do. They found out about you, what your name was, and some obscure information to do with your great-grandfather, then they repeated it back to you to give you a shock, to make out they had supernatural powers. Then—this was the icing on the cake—they vanished in front of your very eyes! Twice Mungo had done that. He knew the short cuts and hiding places. But I'd still find him.

In the morning I cycled out along the Bickleigh Road. I was looking for pineapples on gateposts, and I eventually found them on the left-hand side, about a mile outside the village itself. The wall and gateposts were white, the stone pineapples were the size of rugby balls. I freewheeled to the beginning of the wall, laid the bike down on the narrow verge between the wall and the road and cased the joint. Behind the wall was a hedge that had grown out of control, obscuring the view of the house.

It wasn't that the gates were open. There weren't any gates. I walked between the pineapples, past the hedge and into a garden that looked like a scrubby field that was used for flytipping. Lying stranded on the grass, like dead whales on a beach, were two rusting cars with smashed windows and no tyres. Rusting paint tins were piled in one corner. The house was a modern bungalow, which didn't go with the white wall and the pineapple gateposts. A broken window had been patched with corrugated cardboard. There was still a neon Santa Claus stuck above the front door even though it was August.

The place gave off a bad vibe. I shivered and spun round, expecting to see a nutter holding cheesewire with garotting on his mind. To tell the truth, I almost changed my mind and got the hell out. Then I thought, I'm London. Nothing in Manure Munching Land can faze me. I also wondered whether Mungo wasn't spying on me from one of the cracked and filthy windows. No way would I give him the satisfaction of seeing me chickening out. I took a deep breath, closed my eyes and thought of my dad, then marched up to the front door and rang the bell.

There was no ringing sound inside, which didn't surprise me. The bell probably hadn't worked for fifteen years. I knocked the rusty, cobwebbed knocker. There were panels of warped and cloudy glass in the door. Something dark appeared behind them and bolts slid open top and bottom. The door creaked open and I stepped back so quickly I nearly fell over.

In front of me stood a really fat woman who looked as if she was made entirely of toe cheese. The skin on her face and neck, her wobbly exposed arms, and her stout legs was cheesily greasy and off-white. She wore a flowery dress that was thin and grubby and looked more like a curtain she'd torn down in an abandoned caravan and wrapped around herself.

Her eyes were half swallowed by the skin around them, as if you'd need a coat hanger to hoik them out properly, and she had white hairs growing on her chin. She didn't smell of toe cheese, amazingly. She smelt of something sickly-sweet, as if she had a toilet freshener clamped under each exposed armpit. All in all she looked as if she belonged in a field, digging up unexploded Second World War bombs and eating them.

She said, 'Yeah?'

I said, 'Does Mungo live here?'

She withdrew her head like a tortoise, back into its folds of neck flesh (another coat hanger job). She thought I was taking the piss, I could tell. Why did people down here always think I was taking the piss? She didn't say anything, just shook her head twice, two short shakes, and started to shut the door.

I held out my hand and, feeling stupid, said, 'It's just that—he said his house had pineapples.' I pointed my thumb over my shoulder. 'So a boy called Mungo definitely doesn't live here?'

The bomb-eater said, 'Go away,' and shut the door.

The dark shape remained behind the warped glass, waiting for me to scarper. I walked slowly back across the garden, trying to work it out. When I reached the pineapples I looked back at the house, looking for evidence, stickers in a window, a football, to show that a kid Mungo's age lived there. But there was nothing, except for the dark shape that hadn't moved from behind the glass in the door.

And then I had it. The bastard had scammed me again!

He might look like a div, but the kid I was unfortunate enough to share a first name with was a conman, a manipulator. I had even believed him for a few hours. He had put his fingers in my head and stirred them around just for a laugh, and no one had a right to do that. The next time he tried, there would be a flash of wolf-jaws and Mungo's fingers would be off above the knuckle.

# Chapter 5

Maybe he knew what I was thinking, because Mungo had vamoosed. Every day for the next five days I went out on the bike to look for him. I even risked death by boredom and went into Bickleigh with Mum a couple of times in the hope I might spot him. One thing I did discover: the Smelly Man was back in town. Gavin's Deli had reverted to the One-Stop Poop—or was that a Mungo scam too? But there was no sign of Mungo himself.

After a week he started to seem like a fading dream, and my mind switched to other things—such as the problem of Tally the Tart with the Incredible Moo-ing Cello. Tally was circling closer and closer. Her dad had started turning up at the cottage without warning and once he actually said this: 'I was just passing and thought I'd check up on the plucky maiden who lives in the woods. Make sure the big bad wolf hasn't carried her off yet.'

Mum did not treat this comment with the hysterical laughter it deserved. In fact she smiled so sweetly I almost puked on the spot. I had the horrible feeling that she no longer thought he was the world's biggest

71

bozo, despite the message to that effect tattooed in Day-Glo letters on his forehead.

I was worried about Mum all round. It turned out things had moved on and she couldn't get the design work she'd hoped for. The phone didn't ring. She started drinking wine as soon as the six o'clock pips went on the radio, which was fine except a couple of times she had too much and started crying, and this was bad because I knew that this was exactly what Brian the Bozo wanted, so he could ride to the rescue like the Eighth Armoured Division. And that's exactly what he did. He fixed up a job for her in a charity shop in Bickleigh four mornings and occasional afternoons a week. She sold dead people's anoraks to other dead people for 35p, and got paid about a tenner a day! How sad was that, but at least it got her off my tits.

One morning, as she made her packed lunch to take to work, she said the thing I reckoned she'd been dying to say for days. 'Tally's terribly keen to meet you, you know.'

'Not that again. No and no and no and no.'

'I just want you to have some company. I know you miss London and your friends and I'm really sorry about that. And as soon as you go to school down here in September, you'll make new friends. But in the meantime it's not healthy to be on your own all the time. It's not having a good effect on you, love, is it? Now be honest.'

'I'm not on my own. I've told you. I've got this friend Steve.'

Mum sighed. 'Oh, not that again. Well, I haven't noticed you seeing him lately.'

'He's away.' It was all I could think of to say. 'But he's back soon.'

'Well, when he's back, bring him over.'

I could feel Mum looking sideways at me but I didn't look back at her. 'OK then I will,' I said.

After that conversation I cycled up to the top of the lane and texted Vern and Barry, reckoning that if I could get them down for a couple of days it would knock the Tally idea on the head, or at least put off the horrible moment. They didn't reply so I called them. Vern had his phone switched off but I got through to Barry. 'Hey, dude,' I said when he answered.

'Who's that?'

'Mungo. How ya doin', dude?'

There was a silence, as if Monster had forgotten I existed. Then he said, 'Oh, right. Yeah. All right.'

'What's up?'

'Nothing much.'

I had wanted Monster to fill up the hole I was standing on the edge of, but he was busy making the hole bigger. 'Seen Vern?' I said.

'Yeah, I seen him last night.'

Barry thought he was talking to a dead person, that was the problem. 'Hey,' I said, trying to sound as alive as possible. 'You gonna come down then? It's all right here.'

'Yeah? All right then.'

73

'So we'll sort it, yeah?'

'Whatever.'

But two days went by and nothing happened. And I started to think of Mungo again.


It was easy in the end. Tracking Mungo down started with the noise of raindrops coming down the chimney of my bedroom and falling onto the hearth of the small fireplace. There had been some heavy rainstorms this summer, including the day Mungo and I met, but it had never rained in my bedroom before. When I looked out of the window the rain was so heavy it looked like a white sheet strung across the garden. The storm was soon camped directly above the cottage, the lightning and the thunder fitting together as tightly as Pringles. In my bedroom the ceiling light flickered off, came back on, then went off again. I heard Mum's footsteps downstairs. She'd just got in from the charity shop. She called up the stairs. 'Are you all right, love?'

I said, 'Yeah,' in a bored way, as if I hadn't noticed the violent, exciting weather.

'Some storm, eh? I had to stop the car at one point, the rain was so heavy. The electricity's gone off.'

'I know.'

'It'll be on again in a minute. D'you want a glass of cordial?'

'No I'm all right.'

I heard her footsteps going away, back into the kitchen. I high-fived the window ledge. I hadn't seen anything like this. I knew I had to get out in it. I also knew Mum would try to stop me. She'd say I was crazy, you could get killed by lightning or falling trees. But I didn't care. All I cared about was that the storm made me quiver, like a wolf before it starts to stalk.

I sneaked out by the french doors below my bedroom and ran below window level to the garage. I stood in the shelter of the garage awning and waited, and as I looked out from under my dripping eyebrows the rain let up slightly, enough to see the outline of the garden through the white curtain. I watched a crooked dagger of light plunge into the heart of the lawn, and my heart trembled at the demolition ball of thunder that followed.

The road had turned into a whitewater river. I got on the bike and freewheeled into the river.

Mungo was standing in the road. As I came round the corner he hopped onto the bank and I slammed on the anchors. A squeal of brakes and a plume of rainwater arcing off my front wheel. When I saw who it was I said, 'Hey!' I sounded much more enthusiastic than I meant to, so I followed it up with: 'You tosser.'

'Oh, hello,' he said. His hands were hanging down awkwardly by his sides. He put them on his hips and looked down at me from his superior position on the bank.

I stared back, not wanting to show him the relief that was buzzing in my head. It surprised and annoyed me, that sense of relief. It felt as if someone had opened up my head in the middle of the night and hidden it there without telling me. And only now did I realize it was there.

'You're full of shit,' I shouted. Further up the hill, thunder growled and rumbled and all around the rain hissed into the undergrowth.

Mungo shrugged. 'If you say so.'

'What's your real name anyway?'

'I told you. Mungo.'

'Bullshit. Where did you disappear to that day?'

'Where did *you*?'

'Who told you about my mum's grandfather?'

'Ah,' he said, and lifted up his hands and trembled his fingers, looking like a crazy guy in a movie. 'I've got something to show you.' He put his hand in his shorts pocket, pulled out a small square metal object and held it towards me in the palm of his hand.

'What is it?'

'Take it.'

It was an ancient, battered cigarette lighter with a flip top. They sold them at Camden Lock and they never worked. I offered it back and said, 'So what?'

Mungo said, 'Look at the initials.'

On the side was engraved *M.G.*

'I can't even read it,' I said.

'MG,' said Mungo. 'Mungo Groves. It was great-grandfather's.' He corrected himself. '*Your* great-grandfather's.'

'You are *so* full of shit,' I said. 'I know where to get

76

millions of those.' I chucked it back at him and he snatched at it like a girl, with his hands held up towards his face. It landed among the sodden weeds on the bank. While he bent down to find it, I started laughing, I couldn't help it. 'Man,' I said, 'you are one weird dude.' One of Dad's expressions. I imagined telling Dad about Mungo and his scams. He'd have loved it, wanted me to bring him round immediately. 'Come on, though,' I said. 'How did you find out about my great-grandfather? Was it somebody in the village who remembered my mum?'

Mungo stood up and put the lighter in his pocket. 'You wouldn't believe me if I told you,' he said.

'Too right,' I said, and then hesitated, unsure whether to tell him I'd checked out the great-grandfather story. I decided not to. It would be like giving him power, and he already seemed to have too much. And now he had to give some of that power back to me by telling me what was going on.

'By the way,' I said, 'I liked the scam about where you live. Who's the woman who lives in the pineapple house then? Is she the village moron? How did you do the Gavin's Deli thing? That was clever.'

'I'm not playing tricks on you, if that's what you mean.'

'Yeah right, and I'm Elvis the Pelvis. Look, Mungo, you're taking this too far. Tell me what's going on or— I've got better things to do.'

'There's nothing going on.'

I shrugged and said, 'See you around then.' I lifted my arse on to the saddle and pushed off down the hill.

77

\* \* \*

All those moments, those split-seconds, when life could have gone a different way. If I'd cycled a bit faster so I didn't hear when Mungo called me back; if I'd heard him but ignored him; if I hadn't decided to stop the bike and turn round, giving him one last chance: I'd never have dropped down that deep dark hole.

He ran down the hill, his giant feet splashing through the channels of rainwater, and caught me up. 'What do you want?' I said. 'What's going on? Tell me.'

'If I told you,' he said, 'you wouldn't believe me.'

'Try me.'

Mungo shook his head. 'I'll show you, though. On one condition. You've got to trust me.'

'You promise you'll show me?'

'You promise you'll trust me?'

He looked so serious that I couldn't help laughing. 'You crease me up,' I said.

As we walked up the lane on the far side of the main road, me pushing my bike with one hand, Mungo said, 'How big do you think an ordinary anthill is?'

'Dunno.'

'Go on. Guess.' I shrugged. 'Well, about this high.' Mungo held the tips of his fingers about five centimetres apart. 'In the Happy Valley they're about *this*

78

high.' And he held out his right hand so it was parallel with the road and two metres above it.

'Yeah?' It was difficult to keep a straight face. The guy was completely crazy. But entertaining.

'Just stick with me and do what I do,' he said. 'OK?'

'Aye aye, cap'n.'

At the top of the hill I looked down on tall chimneys and the deep oval of woodland that promised waiting depths and mysteries. We got back on the bike and whizzed off through the spray. Where the road bottomed out, we ran alongside an old iron fence with spikes on top and soon came to two ornate iron gates attached on rusting hinges to brick gateposts about four metres high. The bricks were green and slimy. The gates had rusted to a dark and petrified-looking brown.

Mungo nodded towards the left-hand gatepost and walked round the back of it. Between the gatepost and the fence was a gap, just big enough to squeeze through sideways. Mungo went through first and I fed my bike through to him. My turn. I breathed in and, holding springy branches clear of my trackie top, passed silently into the Happy Valley.

We stood on a track which curved downhill through thick woodland. To either side, the floor of the woods was carpeted with plants that were as bright and green as the moss I'd seen in the bluebell wood with Dad. The trunks of the trees were covered in ivy and the branches were coated with furry green moss. Everything was hushed and the few sounds there were seemed amplified. The steady fall of rain on the undergrowth was like the hum of an electric kettle. Occasionally there would be the plink of an individual raindrop falling from a leaf or a branch to the ground. And the air seemed caressingly soft, as if it was mixed with a soothing essential oil like Mum kept by the bath.

I hid my bike in undergrowth near the gatepost. Mungo said quietly, 'It's best to whisper.'

'Why?'

'It's a nature reserve. That's why you get giant anthills. No one's allowed in except twice a year when university students come on field courses. There's an Irishman with a shotgun patrols it and he'll shoot you if he catches you.'

'Yeah? Blokes can't go around shooting people. They'll get done.'

'Try saying that when you've got a bullet through your brain.'

'Yeah yeah,' I whispered.

We set off down the drive. The storm still rumbled, the rain fell as relentlessly as it had all day. My clothes were sticking to me and the soaking, knee-high weeds were irritating my legs. I noticed handpainted signs nailed high up on trees that were fading and broken and looked as if they'd been there for tens of years. One said, 'Strictly private' and another one said 'No trespassi—'

Mungo saw me looking at the signs and said, 'You shouldn't go in the woods. Kelly's put traps down.'

'Who's Kelly?'

'Irishman with the shotgun. He's hidden these metal traps with razor-sharp teeth that'll take your leg off.' Mungo made claws of his hands and clamped them together. 'Hey, look. Anthill.' He pointed at a cone of earth about a metre high by the side of the track. The rain had drilled it with tiny holes. Mungo rubbed his hands together. 'We'll build a fire when we get there.'

Ahead of us, to the left of the track, a dark, sinister-looking tree rose as high as a block of flats. 'The house is just past that cedar of Lebanon,' said Mungo.

We walked another ten metres and, beyond the paddle shapes of the huge tree's branches, the side of a house became visible. It was a tall house in a dull yellow stone with many windows. Some of the windows showed jagged reflections where broken glass remained. Most were black, indicating the glass had gone completely. High above, seeming to tip towards us through the rain-soaked sky, the tall chimneys that were visible from the hill we'd crossed and, in the middle of the chimneys, a tower with a clock face on it.

Then I heard the noise. Cascading water, a kind of liquid growling. I raised my eyebrows at Mungo and he did that trembling thing with his fingers. 'They only come alive in the rain,' he said.

# Chapter 6

'What do?' I whispered.

'The wolves and owls etcetera.'

'I take my hat off to you,' I said.

'Pardon?'

'It's just something my dad would say, if he was here.'

'Come on and you'll see,' said Mungo and strode off down the path, which swerved to the right and led to a terrace in front of the building. Here the house was leaking, like a giant bucket with holes in the sides. Water poured in great twisting arcs from high up near the roof. Where it hit the ground it threw up fountains of muddy spray. We hopped about, pretending to dodge the spray, pretending we weren't soaked to the bone already.

My eyes scanned along a row of huge ground-floor windows stretching the length of the facade. Above those windows were smaller ones, and above them the places where the water gushed from. Mungo was right. They were animals. They were snarling animals with open mouths and jagged teeth and bulging eyes. Some had raised hackles along their backs. Some had their heads tilted back to the sky. All spewed a never-ending stream of water which churned and fizzed in their mouths as it flew out. They were water spouts carved out of stone.

'Gargoyles,' said Mungo. 'They have to stick out from the building otherwise the water will run straight down the walls. And then the walls will crack because they're made out of limestone.' Mungo had this habit of saying things that were amazing and boring at the same time. 'See?' He pointed. 'Wolf wolf boar dog dog eagle. And round here, look.' He ran to the far end of the house. 'See that crouching little man up there?' On the pointed top of a roof to one side I could just make out a figure. 'A demon. You know why? I'll tell you later. When we've built a fire. Come on.'

Mungo continued round to the back of the house, where the windows and doors were smaller. One of the doors was slightly open. Mungo put his shoulder to it and pushed, forcing a gap big enough for us to squeeze through. I followed him into the Happy Valley House.

We were in a narrow back corridor. The floor was mud, and though there wasn't much light I could make out footprints. The walls were rough-plastered and hard and damp like the walls of a cave. It was freezing. I shivered and felt goose bumps rise on my arms. Mungo led the way down the corridor towards daylight. We went under an arch and passed into a room so big I reckoned you could have fitted our entire house in Gloucester Crescent into it.

The room stretched from the ground to the roof of the building. High, high up, the undersides of the roof tiles were visible. Where tiles were missing, shafts of daylight broke through and in the shafts of light rain fell in a mist that seemed to fade to nothing before it reached the ground. A third of the way up one wall, and a third beyond that, fireplaces floated as if in mid-air. On other walls, doorways opened onto nothing.

'They never got round to putting the floors in,' said Mungo. 'They just disappeared one day and left it.'

'Who did?'

'I'll tell you.'

There was a sudden fluttering of wings and a squeaking in the roof.

'Bats. Greater and lesser horseshoe, and pipistrelle.'

'How d'you know all this stuff?' I said.

But Mungo was on his way to the next room, which was in semi-darkness because planks had been nailed across the windows. I took small tentative steps while Mungo marched around as if he was wearing night-vision goggles.

'Just grab that wood in the corner and drag it into the middle,' he said, 'and I'll light a fire.'

I heard a click and a fizz and the old lighter flared into life in Mungo's hand. He used it to light a candle on the mantelpiece, carried the candle over to one corner and held it over a pile of wood, then returned to the middle of the room and moved the candle in a slow circle. Blackened remains on the floor showed that fires had been built here before.

Mungo scrunched up pages of old newspaper and arranged smaller pieces of wood into a teepee structure above them, then piled the wood I'd brought on top. He knelt down, lit the newspaper and blew on it through cupped hands. The fire took. And now, with something to measure it against, I realized how cold I'd been. I toasted the palms of my hands, then turned round and gave my arse and the backs of my legs the heat treatment.

Mungo rubbed his hands together and said, 'That's better.' Then he picked up the candle, walked over and held it up towards the wall on the right. There were three drawings there, clumsily done with what looked like a burnt stick on the crumbling plaster. The left-hand one was a spiral. The next two I couldn't make out. 'Is that one a brain?' I said.

'Maze. Look.' Mungo put his finger on the entrance to the maze and followed it round, through the ins and outs, to the centre. 'And the other one's an uroboros. A snake eating its own tail. See? There's the head, and the tail comes round in a circle and goes in the mouth. It means eternal life.'

I went back to the fire and shivered. 'Why's this stuff here? It's spooky.'

'A lot of stuff goes on in Bickleigh. Hare coursing. Cock fighting. Wife swapping. Open-air sex orgies.' He pointed at the uroboros. 'Black magic. But it's not out of the ordinary, it doesn't just happen in Bickleigh, it happens everywhere. It's just people, human beings. Human beings do mad and strange things. They always did and they always will.' Mungo shrugged.

'My mum would freak if you said that to her. That's why we came down here. To escape all the weird shit in London. And there's even weirder shit down here.' I laughed. 'What is this place anyway?'

'A madman started building it in eighteen sixty-one.' Mungo walked around the room waving the candle slowly from side to side so it added to the shadow shapes thrown against the walls by the flickering fire. 'He was a Roman Catholic. He wanted the pope to come and live here. He sent him an invitation but the pope never replied. The house got as far as this and then the money ran out. One day in eighteen sixty-nine the workmen just put their tools down and walked out.'

Mungo went over to the mantelpiece and slid an object off it to show me. It looked like a small boomerang. 'Builder's set square, for getting a proper right angle.' He slid it back. 'Been there for nearly one hundred and forty years. The place has been like this ever since. Students come in the summer to study the plants in the Happy Valley. Apart from that no one's allowed in. But they get in. People say the house is haunted but I don't believe it. Why would it be haunted if no one ever lived here?'

I didn't answer. Mungo leant on the mantelpiece. There was silence except for the occasional pop of the fizzling fire and the distant gargling of rainwater in the gargoyles' mouths. I decided to jump feet-first into the silence. 'So what about this book then?' I said.

The question had that Tourette's-like effect on Mungo that I'd noticed before. He started walking up and down, head waggling, fingers fluttering like insects' wings. Twice he turned to me to speak, but didn't say anything. Finally he said, 'Why d'you mention that all of a sudden?'

I wanted to know why the book had given my grandpa bad memories. But I still didn't want to let on I'd asked my mum about it. 'I dunno,' I said. 'I suddenly remembered about it.'

'Have you read it?' He was still really hyped up.

'No way,' I said. 'You're such a bullshitter it probably doesn't even exist.'

He seemed to relax when I said that. 'I haven't read it either,' he said. 'I just heard about it.'

'That's the point,' I said. 'How d'you hear about it? You said you'd tell me.'

'Correction. I said I'd *show* you. That's the next bit. If you're warm enough, let's do it.'

We walked back to the door we had entered by. On the way, as Mungo told me over his shoulder about the demon on the roof, I was thinking: he's lying about the book. Of course he's read it.

'It's for when the devil comes flying over the valley looking for places to visit,' Mungo was saying. 'When he sees a house with a demon on top he thinks, "Oh, they've already got a devil here so they don't need another one", and he flies on to the next house.'

He was playing with the lighter as he walked and talked, flipping the lid backwards and forwards and sparking the flint. He seemed nervous again. At the back door he turned right and we had to clamber over a pile of rubble. On the other side was a courtyard, covered in weeds, enclosed on three sides by the walls of the house and open on the fourth side where it ran into woodland.

There was a strange atmosphere to this cold and still place, as if humans hadn't been here for many years. The rain seemed to fall in slow motion. It fell on the carpet of weeds covering the paving stones, it fell on a thick and rusty chain attached to a ring in the ground, it fell on a stack of ancient roof tiles that looked like flaps of woolly fungus I'd seen growing on dead trees on Hampstead Heath. And it fell on the waist-high brick circle in the centre of the courtyard.

Mungo stood by the brick circle. I knew straight away, without looking down it, it was a well. 'It's deep,' he said. 'Have a look.' He stared at me without blinking, as if assessing me.

I peered over the lip of the well. Slimy sides covered with stuff that looked like green hair. A chill of freezer-cabinet air. I pulled my face away.

'Guess how deep,' said Mungo. I shrugged. 'Try forty metres. I've measured it.'

'Course you have.'

We stared at each other. Electric noise in my head, a feeling that something was happening that I couldn't see or understand. All I knew was, we were both lying about things and we both knew it.

Mungo took out a sheet of newspaper from his back pocket, folded it into a narrow strip, lit one end and held it above the well. I was afraid. I didn't want to get close to the well. But I got close to it anyway. As I knelt on the brick lip to watch the burning paper descending, I felt as if impulses had been smuggled into my head and were now taking control.

Mungo released the paper and it floated down, rocking from side to side, trailing smoke and burnt edges. After a couple of metres the slimy green stones gave way to roughly hacked chalk. My eyes were like a micro camera filming inside a clogged artery. Then the burning paper became a distant point of light, the only star in the sky. I expected, finally, a glint of water but there wasn't one. The burning paper died and the darkness that followed was like waking up from a dream.

'There used to be water in there when I first started coming here but there hasn't been for a few years now,' said Mungo. 'It's dry at the bottom.' He looked at me. 'Well, it's a *bit* damp, but it's OK to sit in. It's even quite comfortable. Cold though.'

Mungo walked past the stack of roof tiles to a door in the wall. He creaked it open, reached round and scooped out a jumble of rope and wooden slats: an old rope ladder. We half-carried, half-dragged it over to the well and laid it on the ground. The slats were slimy; the rope left green stains on my hands. Mungo tied one end to the rusty chain, then we lifted it again and poured it down the well. The way it slid down, making no noise, reminded me of a snake eating its prey.

89

# Chapter 7

All the time the rope ladder was sliding down the well, Mungo was glancing at me, then looking away. I could feel his restless eyes. But I did not look at him. When the ladder was pulled taut against the chain, Mungo gave it a final tug to check his knot was secure. Then he said, 'Right.'

'What?'

He pointed at the well, the ladder disappearing down it. 'Be my guest,' he said.

'What about you?'

'I've got to stay up here.'

It was as if I'd woken up just in time. 'Forget it,' I said. 'I'm not going down there. Certainly not on my own.'

'That's up to you, but then you'll never find out the truth.'

'This is just another scam, isn't it? Why aren't you coming down too?'

'In case anything goes wrong. But if you're afraid of finding out the truth—'

'Bullshit,' I said. 'So let's get this straight. If I go down there now, I'll magically understand everything that's been going on?'

90

'It's not guaranteed, but I hope so. It worked for me. But you've got to want it to work.'

I shook my head. 'This is nuts.'

Another turning point. In theory, even this late in the day, I could have backed out. But the truth was, there was one future for me and it was like gravity. I felt myself falling towards it and—I have to admit— the feeling was half-pleasant.

I climbed on to the lip of the well, felt again the icy presence below. 'I'm only doing this because there's bog all else to do in this boring dump,' I said. 'And if anything happens to me you're in deep shit, OK?'

Mungo was fiddling with the heavy old fliptop lighter again. He passed it over saying, 'Take this, it's dark down there.'

It's surprisingly hard, climbing down a rope ladder to the bottom of a well. My knuckles kept scraping against the chalky sides, my shoulders began to ache with the effort of leaning back to minimize the impact, and the wooden rungs were slimy and treacherous under my trainers. Looking up, I watched Mungo's face slowly slide behind the wall of the well. Was this just another trick? Was he going to leave me down there? I was relieved to see that he looked hopeful and a bit shy, not at all like a scammer who's laughing at his victim.

Soon all I could see above me was a squashed circle of light that grew dimmer and thinner, the deeper I went. Below my feet was complete darkness, a sense of cold nothingness. The sound of my breathing and the squeak of my trainers on the rungs echoed around the damp walls.

I decided that after all, and despite Mungo's bullshit about finding the truth, what Mungo was making me do was just a dare with knobs on. Mungo had dared me to climb down to the bottom of the well and I had called his bluff, which meant that as soon as I had gone to the bottom of the well and climbed out again he would owe me a dare, as well as a proper explanation for his scams. I was trying to think of something suitable for him to do when my legs folded underneath me and I found myself kneeling on the bottom of the well.

I fumbled around me like a blind man: damp earth, a few hard objects that were probably bricks, something round and metallic, maybe the lid of a paint tin. I found a fairly smooth patch and lowered my arse on to it, then leant back carefully till my back touched the rough side of the well. It was a relief, at first, to rest my shoulders and lick my grazed knuckles.

Then the cold and damp began to seep through my clothes, and I decided to stand up. I looped a hand round a rung of the rope ladder and dragged myself upright. And there I stood, in the dark and cold, forty metres down at the bottom of a dry well, under a derelict and forgotten house that was being lashed by a summer storm, as if I was strap-hanging on the Northern Line. I had to admit, Manuresville wasn't boring when Mungo was around. Weird but not boring.

How much time had gone by? It felt like about ten minutes but was probably only two. Was it OK to start climbing back up? I didn't want to seem a wimp by appearing at the top too quickly so I decided to wait a bit longer. The top of the well was no more than a faint, lighter grey in the thick uniform grey that enveloped me. My hands, just ten centimetres in front of my face, were pale suggestions of shape that seemed to have vanished when I blinked and looked again.

I brought out the lighter and flipped the top backwards and forwards a few times, remembering the story Mungo had come up with about the initials engraved on its side. He was a conman, a liar, maybe even a psychopath, but he was a laugh, there was no denying it. Besides, I'd done his dare—or I was in the process of doing it—and I had a sudden, brilliant idea for what he could do in return. After teaching me how to do his scams so I could pull similar ones on other people—Vern, for instance—he would have to go round the neighbourhood with a spraycan changing all the roadsigns that said 'Bickleigh' to 'Manuresville'.

The lighter was cold in my hand. I held it tight to warm it up, then tried several times to light it but my thumb wasn't strong enough to spin the flint mechanism and I gave up, resigned to the darkness. Anyway, it wasn't pitch black. I remembered a much darker place I'd been to: a cave in Barbados, when Dad was producing an album out there and we were staying in a beachfront apartment with its own mini-cinema in the basement and a giant chess-set on the flat roof. While Dad was working, Mum and I did a tour of a cave system deep underground. In the biggest cave, which was as big as King's Cross railway station, they told people to keep dead quiet then they switched the lights off. Wooo. *That* was what you call dark. And scary. Like being an ant at the bottom of a laundry basket.

Silence, except for my breathing. I couldn't see the breath in front of my face but I imagined it. I shivered and massaged my shoulders, trying to rub some heat into me. Now, surely, it was time to get going north-wards. I lifted my head towards the faint lightness far above and called out, 'Mungo!'

Silence.

I cupped my hands round my mouth and called again, louder: 'Mungo!' And then, to myself, as a little reward, 'You complete div.'

There was a noise, shockingly loud in that confined space and after such deep silence. I didn't know what it was at first. A scraping sound, an escaping sound, a sound that shot upwards, leaving a silence behind it that seemed even deeper than before. Uselessly I looked around—up, down, left, right. Then I had a terrible, gut-wrenching suspicion. I reached out, slapping the side of the well. I clawed and clutched as high as I could reach. Trying to be calm and methodical I felt my way round 360 degrees of the well's sides, thinking maybe I'd been disorientated and was looking in the wrong place. Each time I got the same result. The rope ladder had gone.

* * *

I shouted up again: 'Mungoooo! For God's sake!' No reply. I slumped down on the well bottom, too scared now to bother about the cold. Perhaps I couldn't be heard at that depth. Or perhaps I could. Perhaps Mungo heard and couldn't be arsed to reply. Let's face it, I didn't know Mungo well. Perhaps I didn't know him at all. Maybe he *was* a psychopath. Maybe he had escaped from a secure institution. Why, supposing it was him, did Mungo take the rope ladder away? To really scare the Mulhooleys out of me, I guessed.

Well, he was succeeding. From the darkness and silence and cold, ideas started pouring into my head. Maybe, to be fair to Mungo, it wasn't him at all who'd taken the rope ladder away. Maybe it was a cock-fighter or a dogger. A nutter had ambushed Mungo, tied him up and hauled up the rope ladder because that was his idea of entertainment (and let's face it, entertainment took strange forms in the Bickleigh area). Or, even supposing it was Mungo who'd taken the ladder away, which was the most likely explanation, he might have decided to leave the Happy Valley for a few hours, just so I'd get really shit scared. And while he was leaving, the mad Irishman Kelly with the shotgun might catch him and shoot him. Or he'd be run over and killed on the main road. I pictured Mungo dawdling across and a car transporter en route from Southampton docks, loaded with Renaults or Citroëns, comes out of

95

nowhere and flattens him. What then? Only he knew where I was. I'd die. Slowly. Over several days.

I tried to think of other things: Barbados, for instance. Who'd have thought, when Dad was still crashed out after an all-night studio session, and Mum and I used to walk along the beach for breakfast in the Blue Parrot Café—great bacon and fried eggy bread—and the sand was already hot, and the surf was up, I'd end up in this hole in this weird old house built for a pope, near a village that civilization forgot? My life was once as long and wide and warm as that beach in Barbados (without that many beach babes, so far, but I was about to come to that. No way was fifteen too young to start), and now, peering at the grey nothingness that surrounded me, I guessed it was about two metres across, if that. My incredible shrinking world.

Still, I tried to have a good feeling about it. Where I was now was my narrow point, my low point. Literally. From here, the only way was up, as they say. I was going to grow again. My world was going to get bigger and bigger, far exceeding that Bajan beach. Mum would realize she'd made a mistake, moving us down to Manuresville. We'd go back to Camden and I'd return to my old school with my old mates and we'd hang out round the Lock and I'd meet Sue Blass again, and action would follow. And Mum would get plenty of graphic design work and we'd be happy. We'd never forget about Dad, of course we wouldn't, but he wouldn't be a stabbing pain any more, more of a pleasant tingle. All these things were possible. I just had to get out of here. Which was down to Mungo.

I stood up, stretched, tried again to rub some heat into my arms. It felt more than just cold, now, it felt freezing, as if night was falling on an already cold day. I yelled, 'Mungoooo!' again. Or tried to yell. This time the sound seemed to die in my throat. My damp clothes felt stiff and alien, and I suddenly needed a drink badly. I hadn't had anything to drink since well before turning down Mum's offer of weed cordial, what seemed like a lifetime ago. I'd have died for a glass of it now.

Once I realized how thirsty I was, I couldn't get the desire to drink out of my head. The more I tried not to think of it, and made myself think instead about cave systems in Barbados or snogging Sue Blass, the more I saw in front of me a swimming pool filled with Coke and ice cubes and giant slices of lemon the size of beach umbrellas, and me running from over my right shoulder in my swimming trunks and diving right in, and swimming along with my mouth open, drinking the pool dry. You hear about people drinking their own urine, which even now I reckoned I would never do. But the sides of the well were damp, I'd already felt that. If it came to it, I could lick the walls. But not yet.

I had another go at lighting the lighter. For something to do. So I didn't keep obsessing about how thirsty I

97

was. Or what would happen if Mungo got knocked down by a car transporter.

After producing a few sparks, and hurting my thumb, I gave up. I wondered where I would go if I needed a leak. Not that a leak was on the agenda at the moment because I hadn't drunk anything. And this thought made me realize all over again how thirsty I was. I switched the lighter to my left hand and this time it worked. An orange flame billowed from my hand, burning my finger, and the petrol smell made me feel momentarily sick. I moved the lighter in a circle, illuminating a floor of damp earth embedded with bricks and bits of wood and (I was right) an old paint tin lid. Damp glistened on the walls (I was definitely building up to a lick), and, on the far side where the floor met the wall there was a small hole about as big as a golf hole. This was good and bad. Good because if push came to shove I could piss in it. Bad because you didn't know what could come out of it. Rats, for instance.

I extinguished the lighter to conserve fuel and my burnt finger started really hurting, but this was not necessarily a bad thing. I saw a TV programme once about how prisoners and hostages handle extreme situations. (One of the things they said was that women are better at it than men. I'd never wanted to be a girl before.) It was all about mind and body. Even if you're strapped down in the deepest dungeon with three clinically obese blokes sitting on you, so no way are you going anywhere in a million years, you can still travel far and wide in your head. You can float, you can fly, you can win the Champions' League for Arsenal with the last kick of normal time. But it helps to have something for your body to get on with worrying about, while your mind is out there going for it. Preferably something not too bad, like a burning finger, rather than something terrible like a raging thirst.

So now I concentrated everything really bad into that burning finger. How thirsty I was. How freezing. The worry about getting out of here, like where was that stupid manure-munching centre-parted div and didn't he know I wouldn't be his friend in a million years if I lived in a halfway normal world? And most of all the stuff that Mum called 'unresolved', which basically just meant Dad dying.

It worked for a bit but then the thirst came back and wouldn't go away and I knew I had to go for it. I had to lick the wall.


Big mistake. I should have remembered what happened when Vern got me to lick a beer can straight out of the freezer. I left half my tongue on it. The cold wall left my tongue even drier than it was before. I swallowed repeatedly and frantically, trying to summon saliva into my mouth, but there was nothing there. And the taste: like minced rock in cotton-wool sauce. I might have to drink my own piss after all, if I could manufacture any. My finger was hardly burning now. Everything had gone to my mouth.

Then I heard a noise, or thought I did. Mungo was back! He'd had his fun and was lowering the rope ladder back down. I stood up and called out. But there was no follow-up noise. Just silence. It wasn't Mungo with the rope ladder after all. Or maybe it was and he'd stopped lowering it. He'd got my hopes up and now he was dashing them. Or maybe the noise was an animal. Like a rat. Oh no.

I was so thirsty!

I said to myself: concentrate on something else. Anything else. Get your mind out of this hole. And the lid of my mind opened, spilling coloured balls of thoughts.

I wouldn't be here if you hadn't died, Dad. What day is it? Tuesday, a Tuesday in the summer holidays. I would be at Camden Lock probably, if you were still alive. Or maybe we'd be abroad on one of your jobs. In Kingston, Jamaica, hanging out on a verandah overlooking the sea, you allowing me to drink a weak rum punch. But only if I was me.

Hey, Dad, have you thought about what it would be like not to be you, but to be somebody else? Or does that weird thought only come to a person if you get stuck at the bottom of a well, freezing your arse off, with your only means of escape taken away? But then I wouldn't exist at all if you hadn't married Mum and made her pregnant. And you wouldn't have married Mum if you had never met her. (Obviously!) And the only reason you met (because Mum told me) was that you were working in a recording studio in Marylebone with some band or other that never made it, and Elvis Costello was recording an album in the suite next door, the album Mum did the cover for. And Mum was sitting in the hospitality area drinking a coffee one morning and you walked through and asked her if she had a cigarette. She said no. (She also said, to me, she thought you looked quite nice but dressed a bit too young for your age. Maybe you had a previous pair of leopardskin creepers on?) Anyway, that's how you and Mum met. If you hadn't wanted a cigarette, or if you'd had a pack on you and hadn't had to ask, or if Elvis Costello had not been recording that day, or Mum hadn't got the commission to do his album cover, and a million other ifs, I'd have never been born.

That's the last thing I remember thinking before I lost consciousness and entered the nightmare.

# Chapter 8

A banging on the door far below, and when I look out of the bedroom window I see a line of riot police, all togged up in black gear and helmets, so many of them they snake down the street and disappear round the corner towards Camden High Street. I throw open the sash window. The front of the line is at our front door. They are carrrying a battering ram which they swing back and slam into the door, so hard that, three storeys up in my bedroom, the glass of water on my bedside table rattles. I call down, 'Stop it or you'll wake Mum. I'll come down and explain. I didn't mean to kill him.'

But as I lean out of the window I lose my balance and slip forward and there's nothing I can do to stop myself falling head-first. The pavement rushes up towards me and I brace myself for the bone-shattering impact. But there is no impact. I've stopped falling, I'm suspended in mid-air, poised between life and death, and something is coming up towards me, travelling the other way. It's Dad. He smiles but does not stop. I see his creepers pass by my ear and reach out to grab them, but it is too late. I grasp air.

I fall again, and this time do not stop. I'm on my back, splayed like a starfish. Far above, Mungo's face is visible in a circle of light. Is he grinning, or is that just a trick of the light? I can't see where or how far I'm falling. Then I hit something, my fall is broken. I screw shut my eyes, waiting for the pain to kick in, but there is no pain. I've landed on a soft and squishy bed.

I open my eyes. High ceiling, a wall poster showing the planets of the solar system. Tall window. I tip off the bed and go to the window, noticing that my legs ache and there's pain in my arms. Down below, a gravel driveway and a white-painted brick wall. At the entrance to the driveway, two white gateposts with pineapples the size of rugby balls balanced on them. I blink and stare at the pineapples, wondering whether I'm dreaming. Things seem familiar, but I can't remember where from. Then I half-remember. A white wall, pineapples, a grotty brick bungalow. I look around me. But I'm not in a bungalow. This room is on the first floor, and it's big. It has to be part of a large old house.

Footsteps on creaking stairs, a voice—Mum's—calling my name. 'Mungo?' I turn away from the window to face the bedroom door. The door opens and Mum puts her head round. She looks different, with an unfamiliar haircut and a fatter face. 'Mungo, darling, can I have a word before he gets back?'

She calls me 'darling', which surprises me, but I'm relieved because I can tell, from the way she looks and talks, that she doesn't know about the riot police. I nod but can't get any words out. I feel like a ghost.

The sound of tyres on the gravel outside. Mum looks frightened and her head slips back round the door, which closes softly. I look out of the window. A Land Rover Discovery with bull bars on the front that looks like the visor on an American football helmet. I think maybe it belongs to a friend of Dad's, or a client, who's dropping him off. He knows loads of rock stars who dress like tramps but drive in-your-face gas guzzlers.

I'm waiting for Dad to climb down from the passenger seat. I'm waiting for a sight of his drainpipe jeans, his creepers; I'm already half-smiling because I know he'll look up at the house and give me a smile and a wave in case I'm looking. But then I remember something terrible and my heart falls through me like a runaway lift: Dad is dead. At that moment the driver's door opens and a long leg in a green welly dangles out, followed by another leg with welly attached and a gangly body in a pin-striped suit. It is Brian the Bozo.

I duck down below the window, my heart thumping in my chest. I remember the look of fear on Mum's face and feel sick. Crouched there against the wall, I suddenly know, with absolute certainty, that the Bozo is my dad. He always was and he always will be. Somewhere far away, out of grasp, is a memory of something different. A different dad, a different life and world that I was happy in. I reach out for this memory, try to make it real again, but it dissolves like a dream.

\* \* \*

The Bozo—my dad—lifts his hand repeatedly towards my mum, hitting her on the cheek, on the lip, above the eye. A single drop of bright red blood lands on his left green welly. I run towards them, trying to stop him, but I run through them: I am invisible. I scream and they do not hear me.

'Louder,' Dad is saying. He is laughing. We are standing about twenty metres from the magic barn, which he reckons is the optimum distance for the best echo. He starts to say it for me. 'I hate TREES!' he shouts.

And the magic barn shouts back, 'TREES—REES—EES!'

'OK, OK,' I say, then I fill my lungs, tilt back my head and go for it. 'I hate fresh AIR!'

'AIR AIR air,' says the magic barn.

And Dad takes a mega-swing with his right creeper at the bluebells in the hedgerow. 'Hey, kidder,' he says, 'we're all right, me and you. You know that?'

Far far above me, through the fog of dream, came a sound. It was the rope ladder being lowered back down the well. As I opened my eyes and made the transition from unconscious to conscious minds, I felt that panic you feel when you don't know who or where you are. Then I remembered: the well, the rope ladder disappearing, the thirst, the terror, the slipping into a nightmare that was already dissolving like mist, leaving me with a warm feeling that was happy and sad at the same time. And I cried with relief as I followed the rope ladder with my ears, picking up every tap and scrape in its agonizingly slow progress. 'Hey!' I called out. 'Mungo!'

The words didn't sound strong enough to climb all that way out of the well but after a couple of seconds there was a reply: 'Yep.'

The rope ladder now sounded close enough to touch. I stood on tiptoe. Frayed rope brushed my knuckles and I lunged upwards with both hands till I had it. I was clutching the abrasive old rope and the greasy bottom-most rung to me as if they were priceless treasure, tugging till I felt the ladder tighten at the top and I could get my feet on it. Then, before Mungo could change his mind or think of other ways of driving me mad, I started the climb.

Mungo reached down from the lip of the well and held me under the arms. 'One last push,' he said, and I slithered up and over and brought Mungo down with me on to the green wet weeds. He stood up. I carried on lying there. I couldn't move. The sudden daylight was bruising my eyeballs and I closed my eyes. When I opened them, Mungo was leaning over me, staring into my eyes. 'Are you all right?'

I couldn't speak.

'What happened?'

No response.

Finally I had enough saliva to talk. 'Got any water? I'll die if I don't get water.'

Mungo shrugged and looked at the sky. I sat up and for ten minutes I remained sitting among the weeds, in the torrential rain, with my head tilted back and my mouth open. The rain tasted like a three-minute hat-trick by Thierry Henry would taste if it came in liquid form. Slowly it brought me at least halfway back to sanity.

All the while Mungo was standing over me, staring then looking away, shaking his fingers, wanting to talk. A couple of times he started to say something and I waved him away. Finally I closed my mouth, and Mungo said, 'So?'

'So what?' I croaked.

He offered me his hand and pulled me to my feet like footballers do. 'So . . . ' He paused, as if wondering how to put it, then came out with, ' . . . can you remember what your dad's name is?'

'What my *dad's name* is?' I repeated. 'What are you talking about?'

'Just curious. What is it?'

'You nearly half-kill me and you want to know what my dad's called?'

Mungo nodded, looking very serious. 'If you don't mind, yes.'

'Gerry, all right? His name was—is—Gerry. You fucking div.'

'Are you sure?'

There was a flash in my head, the same flash I'd had when I battered the Gobber: a wolf raising its head, eyes bulging, fangs bared. Stepping close to Mungo I screamed in his face, 'What is wrong with you? Why did you take the rope ladder away? Eh? What was that all about? Well, I tell you what.' I pushed him hard in the chest with two fingers. 'Don't you ever try to pull shit like that again or I'll have you. Big time.'

We didn't say a word as we trudged back up the drive. I retrieved my bike from the undergrowth by the Happy Valley gates and we squeezed back on to the road outside and stood facing each other, suddenly awkward. Mungo wouldn't let it go. 'So you're sure nothing happened down the well?' he said.

He wanted my nightmare. He was trying to put his hands in my head again. But not in a million years would I give it to him because, somehow, I knew that telling him would give him power over me. 'You wanna know what really happened down the well?' I said.

'Tell me.' He was so desperate that not just his hands were trembling, his whole top half was jigging about.

'I met Elvis Presley OK? Now fuck off and grow up, Mungo. I'm not playing your games any more.'

I got on my bike and cycled off without offering him a lift, without looking back, ignoring his shouts.

* * *

I dropped the bike in the garage and crept round the back of the house, expecting at any second to hear Mum's voice. Nothing. I let myself in through the french window at the far end. Pools of muddy water ran off my clothes and blobbed on the tiles. I tiptoed up the stairs, trailing water, and into my bedroom. Still no reaction from below. I was hunting in the cupboard for a clean T-shirt and underpants when I heard the door from the living room creak open downstairs.

Mum's voice filtered up the stairs and through the gaps in the floorboards: 'Mungo? Love?'

I shouted down as casually as I could, 'Yeah?'

I pictured her standing at the half-open door, looking down the passage towards the summer room where the french window was. She wouldn't see anything suspicious from there. She wouldn't see the wet floor. Unless she took about three steps forward. She said, 'Sorry, love, I've been asleep for hours. How about a cup of tea? And I bought a nice homemade cake. Date and walnut. Grandma used to make it, remember?'

I relaxed. 'No, I'm all right.'

'What? I can't hear you.' I heard her footsteps coming down the passage. I pulled a face, waiting for the explosion. But there wasn't one, just silence, then Mum said, 'Oh, Mungo, could you come down and give me a hand, love? The rain's blown in through the french doors and the floor's soaked.'

'Down in a minute. I'm just about to have a shower.'

'What, at four thirty in the afternoon?' Mum sounded suddenly suspicious. 'Come down here first, I just need you for a sec.'

'I'm already undressed.' I grabbed the first clothes I could see, sprinted into the bathroom, which was between mine and Mum's bedrooms, and locked the door.

Only now, standing under the shower, did I allow myself to think about what had happened down the well and what Mungo had said. Reluctant as I was to admit it, something amazing as well as terrifying had occurred. Even before the nightmare, my mind had started to fly off in different directions, have these mad thoughts that tumbled out like sweets from a broken dispenser, all these coloured balls of thought flying out through my fingers. And then the end of the nightmare hadn't been a nightmare at all. I was with Dad. That was it! Now I remembered the good bit at the end, and the happy-sad feeling washed over me, until I also remembered Mungo's question when I came up to the surface: what was my dad's name? What business did that div have, knowing about my dad? I shivered in the warm shower, feeling suddenly in danger though what from and why I could not understand.

Standing in my bedroom in my underpants, I was towelling my back when Mum burst in without knocking. 'Please can you give me a hand, Mungo, as I asked you to,' she said.

'Please can you knock first. I'm still getting dressed.'

'Mungo, why are you hanging around in the bathroom and having showers in the middle of the afternoon?'

'It's not a federal offence, is it?'

'Didn't you even notice the rainwater in the summer room? You've trailed it all the way up the stairs. You're spending too much time alone. You're too wrapped up in yourself. It's not healthy, Mungo.'

I laughed at her then. If only she knew where I'd been, what I'd done.

'It's not funny either.' Then she noticed my knuckles. 'What happened to your hands? What have you been doing?'

I looked down at my hands and put a surprised expression on. 'Dunno. They just went like that. I must have been doing something.'

'You must have been doing something a little too vigorously, if you ask me. Now put the rest of your clothes on and come downstairs and help me. And open a window. It smells musty and—' she couldn't think of the right word for a second— 'unpleasant in here.' The phone rang in the kitchen and as Mum went out of the door to answer it she said, 'Get moving.'

'*Jawohl!*' I said to the back of the door, and did a Hitler salute.

When I got downstairs Mum was spreading newspapers over the wet floor of the summer room. 'Some storm, eh?' she said. 'The rain blew in right through the doors. Can you fetch the mop and bucket?'

When I came back with the mop and bucket she'd finished laying the newspaper. 'Now, Mungo,' she said, 'I've got some things to tell you. I've decided I'm going to re-decorate the cottage. From top to bottom. I don't feel I can move on with your grandma and grandpa's stuff all around. It's like living with ghosts. So I'm going to bite the bullet and clear a lot of stuff out and repaint the rooms and generally make it more cheerful for us both. OK?'

I shrugged. 'Fine by me.'

'The thing is, do you want to help? Earn some money by doing some clearing and painting?' I started to shake my head. 'Why don't you want to help?' She folded her arms across her chest and stared at me. I sensed I was about to get a lecture on how it would be good for my character to paint a wall.

No I wasn't. I had an idea, and I knew I was right. I said, 'Don't tell me. The Bozo's got something to do with this.'

Mum didn't know how to answer so she said, 'Don't call him that.'

'He has, hasn't he?'

'Brian did say he would help, yes. So what?'

'So, a) he's a bozo, b) he's trying to get off with you, c) he's married to Felicity Flapdoodle, in case you hadn't noticed. And d)—' I had a flash from the nightmare. The Bozo's fist going into Mum's face. '—he's a sicko.'

Mum squashed the mop down in its bucket and leant heavily on it, not looking at me. 'Lift up the newspaper please,' she said. She was mad as hell. As she mopped where the newspaper had been, she said, still without looking at me, 'You're overstepping the line, Mungo. I've a good mind not to give you the other news.'

'What other news?'

'That was Vernon Crottall's mother on the phone, confirming that Vernon and Barry would be thrilled to bits to come and stay next week. God knows why, with you in this mood.'

# Chapter 9

I immediately felt guilty as hell for being horrible to Mum, when all the time she'd been fixing for Vern and Monster Mash to come down. The plan was for them to get the train from Waterloo in four days' time and Mum and I would meet them in the Skoda at Bickleigh station. I texted them about it, said I had this amazing thing to show them, meaning the Happy Valley and the well. Because that was the plan. I was going to send them down the well. I wasn't going to take the rope ladder away, that would be too much. But I wanted them to have the same experience I'd had, before the nightmare/dream, of the lid of the mind opening and coloured balls of thought chucking themselves out.

I'd been thinking a lot about what had happened and I wasn't nearly as frightened as I had been. The well had some unusual properties, that was all, like the magic barn. It had seemed to defy rational explanation, but Mungo was just clever at manipulating people's feelings, making things seem stranger than they really were. That way, a person who was basically a div and a dork could hold power over people. But

I didn't need Mungo. I could play the same tricks on Vern and Monster, hold power over them, make them respect me again. Strictly for a laugh, of course.

Vern texted back saying he was going to bring some drugs. He wrote it DRUGZZZ. I texted back saying we wouldn't need drugs, it was going to be amazing anyway. Vern scared me sometimes. I didn't know what he meant by drugs. It might just be his mum's headache pills, or it might be something much worse that he had nicked from his mum's surgery. I tried not to think about it.

In the meantime I tried to be extra nice to Mum. I even offered to help a bit with the redecorating. I stopped referring to Brian Boland as the Bozo. In fact I stopped referring to him full-stop. And I made a shopping list from a book called *Thai-licious!* for a Thai green chicken curry I was going to make as a surprise for Mum. The list included Thai aubergines, chilli peppers, fish sauce and lemongrass. Complicated and obscure foodstuffs for Manuresville in general and certainly out of the question for the Smelly Man. But I thought I'd go there anyway, just to wind him up.

I was also curious about Gavin's Deli. How had Mungo pulled that scam? There was only one explanation I could think of: it wasn't Mungo's scam at all. The answer lay in television. A company was making a TV series about a gay guy called Gavin who moves to Manuresville to open a delicatessen. And they'd borrowed the Smelly Man's rat hole to film it in. Before filming each episode the set designers changed the SM's asphyxiation chamber into Gavin's Deli. That was how everything had looked so clean and shiny when Mungo and I were there: the garlic and salami and the glistening, bright green olives in their tubs were plastic. Hidden cameras were rolling and Gavin—'Gavin', the actor playing him—was in character. When filming was over they collected up all the plastic produce and the plastic leafy branches in the windows, and changed it back. That was my theory and I was going to ask the Pungent One if it was true. After I'd asked about lemongrass etcetera.

'Aubergines from Thailand?' said the Smelly Man. 'I've got aubergines from Holland.' He picked up a thing that looked like a dead mole. The purple skin had gone brown and wrinkled.

'No, they're completely different from ordinary aubergines,' I said. 'They're small and greeny-white and you put them in things like Thai green chicken curry.'

The Smelly Man had that droopy cardigan on again. The shop smelt of the usual: cigarettes, rotting vegetables, and toe cheese. He narrowed his watery eyes at me. The fingers of one hand were flapping backwards and forwards as if he had a nervous twitch. 'You've been in before,' he said.

'Yeah.'

'What was it that time?'

'Chorizo.'

'Go on. Get lost.'

I couldn't believe it. 'What?'

'I'm not playing your games. Get out.'

His twitching hand reached down and brought out a thick stick which he laid on the counter. It was smooth, wooden, with a black leather handle and a strap: a policeman's truncheon.

Talk about Wild West. This was wilder than Camden. I backed off towards the door and reached behind to put my hand on the handle so I could make a quick exit. 'OK, no problem,' I said. 'Can I just ask you a question? When are they filming the next episode of *Gavin's Deli*? Cos maybe they'll pay you enough to retire, then a real-life Gavin could take the shop over and sell real-life Thai aubergines, and chorizo and olives and other decent stuff, then I wouldn't have to knacker myself cycling all the way into Bickleigh cos your shop's crap and smells like a sewer.'

The Smelly Man was deceptive. He was breathing heavily and his chest was clanking but he turned into a blur as he came round the counter. I had no time to slip round the door. He raised the truncheon and brought it down hard towards my arm. He'd have broken it, I reckon, if I hadn't just managed to pull it out of the way. His eyes were bulging in my face, the truncheon was thwacking into the wall, then I managed to get the door open and escape. 'Oi,' I shouted. 'You can't do that, you maniac. I'm going to report you.'

That malodorous nutter could be locked up for what he'd just done, is what I was thinking as I cycled along the verge of the main road. Adults couldn't go around doing violence to kids for no reason, or even for the minor reason of taking the piss. But I knew Mum wouldn't want to get involved in anything like that. She would reckon I had done something to provoke him. And she wouldn't want to alienate local people. She'd say it was different down here, different rules applied and I'd better get used to it. Well, I could apply my own rule in that case. I stopped to text Vern, asking him to bring a spraycan when he came down. The Smelly Man's shop was about to receive some re-decoration.

You'd think there'd be one shop in Bickleigh, among all the shops offloading hearing aids and stairlifts and walking frames to a vast and grateful audience, selling Thai aubergines and the like. But no. I went to the Bickleigh deli, I checked out the minimarket, I even asked in the chemist's because I saw a woman through the window and she was fat and looked like she enjoyed hoovering up food at every available opportunity. But the woman in the chemist said there was no demand for obscure foreign food in Bickleigh. She said the butcher's did brilliant pork, celery, and leek sausages and why didn't I get those? I almost told her to shove her sausages where the sun don't shine except that was probably her hobby anyway because what else was there to do in Bickleigh?

I gave up and wheeled my bike round to the charity shop. I suddenly felt tired. I was going to put the bike in the back of the Skoda and cadge a lift home off Mum when she finished in half an hour. She wouldn't mind because we were new best friends. That was the idea.

I'd never been in the charity shop before. If I'd known who was there I'd never have gone in.


Mum was behind the counter and she was being sickeningly nice to a manure muncher. She was even starting to look and sound a bit like one herself, which wasn't all that surprising considering she'd started out as one. She was wearing a horrible hairy checked jacket that made her look like someone whose job is to warm toilet seats for female royalty. And her voice had turned—not exactly posh, but it had already lost quite a bit of London.

After blushing, she half-waved at me over the manure muncher's shoulder and I smiled and shrugged, to mean, Take your time, I'll just have a look round, and she gave a little nod and carried on talking. It was cool sometimes, the way Mum and I could say quite complicated things just by nodding and blushing and waving and shrugging. I decided that when we got back to The Hollow I would light some candles and put on some decent music on the downstairs sound system—the Elvis Costello album, for instance, that Mum had done the cover for and which was the reason she'd met Dad.

The manure muncher left, saying, 'Shall we see you at the talk tonight? It promises to be extremely interesting.'

And Mum said, 'I'll certainly do my best.' When the woman had left, Mum said, 'Hello, love, what a nice surprise.'

'I was just—Can I get a lift home off you? I'm a bit bushed.'

'Of course you can.'

And then a woman came out from the back carrying an armful of clothes in her big blubbery arms and Mum said, 'Oh, Mungo, this is Rosemary Strickland.'

And I looked and I couldn't believe it. It was Mrs Toe-Cheese.

'Rosemary, this is my son Mungo.'

Mrs Toe-Cheese dumped the armful of clothes on a pile of black bin bags and wiped her forehead. Her cheesy skin had turned pink and she was sweating. She looked at me properly then. Her bomb-eating mouth fell open and those eyes zoomed out and in until she had me in focus. 'Mungo?' she said.

'Hey,' I said to Mum, 'forget the lift. I don't really want to hang around so—'

Mum said, 'It's OK, I can be done here in ten minutes. That'll be all right, won't it?'

'No, really. See you later.'

On the way back to the cottage my mobile vibrated in my pocket and I stopped the bike to find a text from

Vern. It said, 'NAH WIMP DRUGZZ U BETTA BLEVE IT'. I sent him one back saying, 'forget drugs dont forget spraycan'.

When I got back to the cottage I got a couple of mugs out and put the kettle on to boil while I waited for Mum to return. I was wondering whether Mrs Toe-Cheese had recognized me. The way she had looked at me, the way she had said, 'Mungo?' the answer to that had to be yes. If so, had she said anything to Mum? Also, did she have a kid, and did he happen to be called Mungo?

When I heard the Skoda scrunching into the driveway I flicked the switch to bring the kettle back to the boil. I wanted to be occupied when Mum came into the kitchen.

She dumped the bags on the work surface and I said, 'Cup of tea?'

'Thanks.' She flicked off her shoes so she was barefoot and sat down at the kitchen table. 'What happened to you?'

I put Mum's mug in front of her on the table. 'I felt like the exercise.'

'You were "bushed" thirty seconds before that.'

'No, it was—so who's Mrs Strickland then?'

'Miss. She's the sister of the local policeman. I just dropped her off. Her usual lift couldn't make it.' Mum looked at me over the top of her mug. She held the mug close to her mouth with both hands, extending her lips like a chimp's to drink.

'Has she got any kids?'

121

'No. What have you been up to today?'

And I knew, the way she changed the subject, that Mrs Toe-Cheese, besides not being that dangerous div's mother, had kept shtum about me. A bag of wine gums for old Toe-Cheese. I said, 'Oh, nothing much, just getting assaulted by a nutter with a truncheon.'

Mum put the mug down and looked concerned. 'What are you talking about?' I told her what happened with the Smelly Man, and she relaxed. 'Teach you to keep that fast mouth of yours zipped more often,' she said when I had finished.

I couldn't believe her attitude. 'Adults can't go around assaulting kids like that,' I said. 'Not any more.'

'He didn't actually assault you, did he?'

'Only cos I pulled my arm away. He tried to.'

There was the sound of tyres scrunching on the gravel of the driveway. I went over to the window and looked out. The bozomobile, complete with Bozo. 'It's Brian,' I said, with an effort. Then a flash of the nightmare returned. I saw him arriving outside the Pineapple House. I saw his fist crashing into Mum's face. I knew I was being unfair—even the Bozo couldn't be blamed for what I happened to dream in the privacy of my own head—and I resolved to behave, for Mum's sake.

Mum went to open the front door for him. I listened out to hear whether they kissed but I wasn't sure. When the Bozo came into the kitchen he said, 'Hello, young man. Are we shipshape?'

In my head, several football stadiums full of people were busy being sick but I just said, 'Yes, thank you.'

The Bozo put a bag on the kitchen table and Mum took out the contents: small tins of paint. Mum clicked them into a line and said, 'Brian's brought some samples round.'

'Oh right,' I said. 'Jolly good.'

'Get the place brightened up,' said the Bozo. He rubbed his hands together and raised his eyebrows at me.

'I was just about to tell you,' Mum said to me. 'I'm going out tonight. I'll do you some spaghetti before I go. Is that OK?'

'No problem. Where are you going?'

The Bozo said, 'A talk at the Women's Fellowship on "The Wells of Old Wessex".'

'What?' I said, a bit too loud. I looked from the Bozo to Mum, and they looked at me, and I felt myself blush.

'What's the matter?' said Mum.

'Nothing,' I said, thinking, for a split second, they knew something. I changed the subject. 'Is—' I almost said 'Old Flapdoodle'. 'Is your wife going to be there too?'

'Er . . . well, Felicity organized it originally but she's not feeling on top form at the moment so—'

Mum said hurriedly, 'It's actually a very interesting subject, Mungo. A lot of old houses round here have very deep wells.'

'Really?' I said.

The Bozo said, 'We have one at Hedge End Hall House actually, although it's blocked off now. Mrs Plunkett-Snipe's done a study of them.'

123

I said, 'Is she related to Mrs Plunkett-Strawberry?'

The Bozo said, 'Who?'

Mum shook her head at me. It was such a little shake it was more like a vibration, but I saw it. 'Mungo's being silly,' she said. To me she said, 'What sauce do you want with your spaghetti? There's bolognese or carbonara.' She brought out two jars from her shopping bags.

'Bol.'

Mum got some saucepans out and started fussing about, putting her shopping away in the fridge and in cupboards and starting my spag bol at the same time.

The Bozo sat down and fiddled with the paint pots. He said to the paint pots, 'Wells are actually fascinating things. You can date a house from the method of construction of its well. And some of them are supposed to have secret passageways and tunnels leading off them which means they were jolly useful for hiding things down.' He laughed suddenly and loudly, as if he'd cracked a sidesplitter.

'Like what?' I said.

'Contraband.'

'What's that?'

Mum said, 'Illegal booty.'

The Bozo said, 'So the excise men wouldn't find it.'

I said, 'Oh, like crack cocaine.'

Mum threw the fridge door closed and said, 'Mungo.' The way she said it, very short and tight, meant: enough already. That's how Dad would have put it. 'Would you like to get the grater and grate yourself some cheese?'

I knew I was pushing it. Maybe, if I did it once too often, she'd pack me off to live with a relative I'd not heard of yet, an uncle in Norway, say, who belonged to a strict religious sect and went in for part-time kiddie fiddling. Even Manuresville would be preferable. Just. I was certainly putting the visit of Vern and Barry in danger. But I couldn't help it when the Bozo was around. He was such a dork I couldn't believe it. I took the grater off its hook and Mum handed me a lump of Cheddar and a bowl.

'Haven't you got any proper Parmesan?' I said, but Mum just bulged her eyes and shook her head, indicating that she would explode if I didn't zip it.

Silence. The Bozo was flicking paint pots, I was grating cheese, and Mum was bending down to check how high the gas was under the bol sauce. No one was saying anything. So I dived in.

'Hey, Mum,' I said, 'so what was this book about by my great-grandfather?'

'Why are you bringing that up now, Mungo?' She jerked her head at me. More eye-bulging.

'Just interested.'

'Is this something I should know about?' said the Bozo with a sickly grin on his face. 'Did an ancestor go by the name of Dickens, by any chance?'

'Good heavens, it's nothing like that,' said Mum. 'It's nothing really. It's just a small scientific book from years ago. More like a pamphlet, in fact. Mungo's latched on to it for some—'

I said, 'If it's nothing, how come it gave Grandpa bad memories and he chucked it?'

'Mungo, stop it right there! You're determined to be clever and I won't have it.'

'OK, already! Keep your knickers on, dude!'

More silence, the Bozo sweating a bit as if he'd walked in on Mum on the pan. Then he said, 'Sherwood Green is an interesting hue.' He said 'hue' in an exaggerated way, as if he thought it was a hilarious word.

Mum jumped in quickly, just in case I was about to be sarcastic, which I wasn't. She said, 'Yes.' Then she said to me, 'What else did you do today, Mungo?'

'I told you. I got attacked by the Smelly Man.'

Mum said to the Bozo, 'He means the shop on the main road. He was cheeky and got short shrift in reply.' She said to me, '*Please* don't call him that, dear. I meant after—'

The Bozo said, 'Old Maurice?'

I said, 'Short shrift?'

Mum said, 'Perhaps people should do that kind of thing more often.'

I said, 'Mum! You're so right-wing these days, I can't believe it.'

Mum gave me her X-ray-eyes stare. 'Would you like a glass of cordial, Mungo? You must be thirsty.'

'No, thanks. Weed cordial is not my cup of tea.' I glanced at the Bozo to see if he was laughing at my joke but he hadn't even got it.

# Chapter 10

Enter Vern and Barry, trailing London arsiness. Not. I was standing on the platform when the train came in. Mum was waiting in the car in the carpark. I watched the windows flash by, getting slower and slower. Then the train stopped with a groan, the doors clunked open, and the train turned into a fish with ten gills. A few people got off: a woman with a shopping trolley, a dead bloke with two walking sticks. But no Vern and Barry. I ran along the platform, peering into the carriages. There were just a few people left on the train, reading newspapers or sleeping with their mouths open. No last-second Camdenites.

Typical. They'd probably got the wrong train and were on their way to Brighton. Or, knowing Vern, he'd woken that morning and thought, What's the point in going to see a dead person in the village that time forgot? So he'd texted Barry and they'd arranged to meet at the Lock instead. They didn't care about me. I was a dead person.

I watched the train bloke blow his whistle on the platform and lift his white table tennis bat. The yellow end of the train got smaller and smaller as it disappeared deeper into Manure Munching Land, and I shook my head to flick a tear off my cheek. I suddenly felt angry. I wasn't going to feel sorry for myself. Never be a victim, Dad used to say, and I wasn't going to start now. Somehow I'd—then Mum was coming down the platform waving her mobile, and I paused the thought. 'Vernon's mum's just been on,' she shouted. 'They're running late. They're on the next one, which means we have an hour to wait. Which is actually bloody annoying. I'm going to nip to the shops and the library. What'll you do?'

I tried not to look too relieved. 'Oh, right, I'll just hang out in the car.'


Mum got back to the car ten minutes before the next train was due. She sat looking at paint charts and ignoring me.

'So what's the big deal about this book?' I said, looking at the side of her face to gauge her reaction.

Mum sighed and closed her eyes. 'I wish I'd never mentioned it,' she said. 'There is no big deal, all right, Mungo? End of story.'

'So why did it give Grandpa bad memories?'

'Because—' Mum hesitated. 'Because his father, my grandfather—Mungo Groves—was a very eminent man, quite famous and very well respected, and then things went wrong for him. He didn't have a very happy end to his life.'

'Why?'

'He ended up in a sort of home.'

'A loony bin?'

Mum sighed. 'My son has such finesse. He wrote the book towards the end of his life and it reminded your grandad of that unhappy time, that's all. So he got rid of it. Satisfied?'

'No. What was the book about?'

'Scientific theories, about the universe and things like that as far as I remember. Now do you mind? I just need to check these charts out.'

The level crossing gates began to flash and hoot. I opened the passenger door. Mum looked up and said, 'Let's all have a nice day, shall we? What have you got planned?'

'Nothing much,' I said, and got out of the car.

Back on the platform, I thought at first that Vern and Barry had missed this train too. The usual assortment of losers got off, the platform jobsworth blew his whistle, and I turned back towards the exit, feeling my eyes beginning to sting again. Then there was some sort of ruck. The platform bloke yelled, 'Shut the door! Get back on the train!'

I turned back. A long way down the platform, a door was opening. Two kids were falling out of the carriage, with backpacks and a big bottle of drink coming with them. One of them was shouting: 'Hang on. Is this—? Where are we?' The kid shouting was Vern, the other kid was Barry. I knew what we had to do.

I ran along the platform. I had just scored a goal. The line painted along the platform was the touchline at the Emirates Stadium. Vern and Barry were my team mates. They had just provided me with the goal—a quick one-two between them, a low cross, me flicking a diving header into the bottom corner. I ran right up into their faces, pressed my forehead forward and held out my arms so we could interlink and frown and do that goal celebration thing.

Vern stepped back and giggled, flapping his hands as if he was fending off killer bees. 'Hey, man. Back off, yeah?'

Barry was looking at the ground. He said, 'Vern's a bit wasted.'

I dropped my hands by my sides. I felt foolish, like I had after doing the Statue of Liberty in front of Mungo. 'Oh no,' I said.

Barry said, 'He's been in the toilet doing this stuff he nicked off his mum.'

Vern giggled and did a slow motion mid-air punch. 'Oh yes.'

I picked up the drink bottle and Vern's backpack. 'What sort of stuff?'

'I'll give you some later.' Vern patted the front pocket of his jeans and winked at me.

'Look, just hold it together for my mum, OK? We've got to go back to the cottage first. Then we can go out.'

'What we gonna do? Cow rustling?' Vern giggled again.

Barry said, 'Vern!' and I knew by the way he said it, it was something they'd been discussing on the train. They'd been staring out of the window at all the fields and cows and they'd said, What the hell is there to do down here? Apart from cow rustling. And they'd both laughed, and Barry had said, Don't say that to Mungo, he'll get pissed off. And the first thing Vern had done was say it to me. Typical Vern.

Vern behaved himself in the car. It was amazing how he could do it. One second a spaced out wreck, next second young Mr Respectable. When they got in, Mum said, 'Morning, boys. Lovely to see you again. Mungo's been so looking forward to it.'

And Barry just said, 'Hello,' and looked at his trainers but Vern said, 'Lovely to see you too, Mrs McFall.'

And Mum said, '*Thank* you, Vernon.'

He was a charmer, Vern.

I sat in the back with Vern, and Barry sat in the front next to Mum. It was sunny and windy. We had the car windows open and the noise of the Skoda bounced back off the hedges as we drove up the lane towards the cottage. The wind blew our hair about, especially Vern's. Mum tried to shout a few questions to Vern about what war zone his dad was reporting from at the moment, but no one could hear properly so she gave up and we didn't speak. I kept looking at Vern's backpack, wondering if the spraycan was in there, whether he'd remembered to get one.

It was weird to see Barry and him again. They were

131

the same and different. Vern's hair was quite a bit longer, Barry looked a bit fatter. But it wasn't just that. They were like replicants of themselves. They were recognizable, they talked the same, they wore the same clothes. But they weren't quite them. They couldn't look me in the eye, which was a replicant giveaway. And they were looking (I mean looking without looking—glancing) at me as if I was a replicant too, a replicant of me made out of straw and cowpats. I had the feeling that this was somehow to do with Mungo. Me meeting Mungo had changed me, given me a secret they didn't know, and Vern and Monster sensed the change. What would they make of Mungo if they met him? They would laugh at him, and it was true, he looked like the sort of out-of-town mong who would go to Camden for the day and buy a wrap of dried herbs for thirty quid thinking it was marijuana. But there was something else about him—the crazy tricks— that was very cool in its own way. Half-mong, half-maniac. Maybe I was becoming like him. Vern and Barry were still kosher Camden but I was halfway through the transition into a cow rustler.

It was only hitting me now how much my life had changed in the few weeks since Vern and Barry were my permanent mates. There were only four weeks left to the end of the summer holidays. I'd already been to see my new school, which looked like an army barracks—even Mum said that—and I couldn't see myself fitting in there at all. Maybe I'd even have to grow a centre parting and wear crap clothes about

132

twenty years out of date so I didn't stand out. And then I'd be embarrassed ever to see Vern and Barry again, or if I did they'd call me Manure Muncher. And it would be true. Slowly, as in a sci-fi film where you don't notice things at first, I would have turned into someone else. Soon I would be like Mungo, I would start thinking bigoted thoughts about gay people.

Then I got angry inside. I would show them there were more things to do down here than cow rustling and insulting gays. I would blow them away with a house and a well.


We dropped their backpacks at the cottage and I said we were going out. Mum asked where and I said I didn't know, we'd just hang out. 'Well, don't do anything stupid,' she said. 'You're not in Camden Town now you know.' Vern giggled.

We had to walk because I didn't have one spare bike let alone two. Vern said, 'Isn't there a bus?'

I shook my head and strode out of the driveway. 'We're going to this amazing place. You won't believe it. It's a bit of a schlepp but it's worth it.' I turned round and waited for them to catch up, then I said to Vern, 'Hey, did you get the spraycan I texted you about?'

'Come again, my friend?'

'The spraycan.'

'You never texted me about no spraycan.'

'What's that noise?' said Barry.

I listened. I couldn't hear anything, apart from birds

but I was pleased to have something to distract me from thinking that Vern was a nasty, useless liar. 'What noise?' I said.

Barry stopped and tilted his head at the hedge. 'There.'

'What? That *jjzzzzz-jzzz* sound? Grasshoppers.'

Vern elbowed Barry and said, 'I hereby inform you you have failed to pass the entrance exam for the honorary company of cowpat worshippers.'

We carried on walking. 'So what's happening?' I said to Vern.

'Nothing much. Oh yeah. You know Sue Blass?'

'Yeah, course.'

'Oh, yeah, I forgot about you and her.' Which was a lie. He'd been jealous as hell.

'She's a teasy-arsed bitch,' said Barry.

'Why?' I said.

'Cos she's giving it out big time with Barry's brother,' said Vern, and looked at me and giggled.

'But he's twenny-two,' I said.

'Yeah. So?'

'He's twenny-three,' said Barry.

We had to stand up on the verge while a car went by. Another one came two minutes later and we had to stop again, which pissed Vern off. The car was a Discovery. It was the bloody Bozo. 'Oh no,' I said, and kept my head down.

'Who was that?' said Vern.

'Just this bloke who fancies my mum. He's a bozo.'

'I just gave him the finger,' said Vern.

'Oh great.'

We carried on a bit and Vern said, 'This is boring.' Barry kicked a stone.

I could have whacked Vern one. Bam. That was for forgetting the spraycan and not caring a shit. Double-bam. That was because he only told me about Sue Blass to wind me up, and anyway there should be a law against twenty-three year olds sniffing around the Sue Blasses of this world. But I stayed calm. 'Just stick with it,' I said. 'It'll be worth it, promise.'

Barry toe-ended another stone.


It was the wrong place, I knew that as soon as we reached the top of the hill. There was the valley all right, spread out in front of us like a green and yellow dish and shimmering in the heat haze. Vern put his hands on his hips and said, '*Lord of the Rings* or what?' It was his way of saying it was cool but I hardly noticed because I'd already seen what was at the bottom of the hill: the metal barns and the security fence of the Bozo's global manure emporium.

Barry said, 'What's that noise?'

Vern said, 'Oh no not again. It's probably a vel-ocoraptor coming to get you Barry cos they love greasy hair. You get 'em down here, don't you, Mung?'

'Yeah. Big yellow ones.'

Vern laughed but I was too busy scanning left and right, trying to work out where the road to the Happy Valley must be.

'No, listen,' said Barry. 'It's like squawking.'

Vern said, 'It's chickens.' He flapped his elbows in and out and made chicken noises. 'Hey, you know what, there are more chickens than people in the country. Chickens rule the roost.' Then he realized he'd made a joke and said, 'Geddit? I know *you* don't, Barry, you div. Where's this place we're going to? I'm bored as doggy-do, speaking personally.'

'Look, guys,' I said. 'Change of plan, yeah? Let's just go back to the cottage and play music, yeah?'

Vern said, '*Que?*'

I pointed down the hill and said, 'It's way over there. I didn't realize it was so far. You really need a car to get there and it's not so great anyway.'

'Oh right,' said Vern.

Glancing at Vern to make sure it was OK to speak, Barry said, 'This is bullshit.'

'Correction,' said Vern. 'This is Bullshit-shire. Get me out of Bullshit-shire before I turn into a bull-shitting mong.'


On our way back to The Hollow I walked on ahead of Vern and Barry so they couldn't see my face, which felt tight and red, with a lower lip that I couldn't stop trembling every so often. When this horrible embarrassing day was over, and the mates I had lost for ever were back on the train to sanity and civilization otherwise known as London, I was going to have to take drastic action. I was going to escape before the damage to my brain that country life and loneliness was inflicting became permanent.

I stepped on the bank to let a car go by. Behind me, Vern and Barry had some sort of a ruck with it that I didn't see. The car bipped its horn and Vern shouted, 'Dozy bumpkin.'

Vern and Barry now had all the proof they needed that I was dead, and they were alive. You could tell they were alive by how quietly they whispered, and how loudly they laughed. And they were right, I had died inside. But it still wasn't too late. I thought again of what Dad had said about not being a victim, and I knew what I had to do.


Vern said, 'Hey, guess what, guys?' He pulled a bottle out of his jeans pocket and rattled it: *shuh shuh shuh*. 'Medicine time.'

We were sitting in my bedroom playing music. Mum was still at the charity shop and Vern had just said again that he was bored as doggy-do. He held up the jar.

'What is it?' I said.

'Hey, need to know basis, OK? All you need to know is, it works.'

'How many d'you take?' I asked.

'Try three for maximum lift-off.'

I thought: at least this'll be quicker than Plan A.

# Chapter 11

Vern unscrewed the top of the bottle. I held out my right hand and Vern shook three pills into my palm. 'I'll go and get some water,' I said.

Down in the kitchen I put the pills on the work surface while I filled a glass. I looked at the pills, picked one up, put it to my mouth. Maybe it would make me feel better. Maybe it would make Vern and Barry like me again. My hand was trembling, my throat felt dry. I was worried Vern would follow me down and stand over me to make sure I swallowed all the pills. I listened but heard nothing beyond the faint thump of the CD player in my bedroom. I clicked the pill back down next to the other two and took a sip of water. Then I acted quickly, before I had a chance to change my mind.

Sweeping the pills off the work surface and into my open hand, I executed a Thierry Henry pirouette that took me across the kitchen, swung my foot down on the pedal of the pedal bin, and dunked the pills down among the breakfast toast crusts. Then I took the glass of water up to the bedroom wondering if Barry was going to be stupid enough to actually swallow his.

Barry was sitting on the edge of the bed looking unhappy, holding the pills in his outstretched hand. Vern nodded for me to give the glass of water to Barry, then raised his eyebrows and said, 'I hope Mungo wasn't a naughty boy and threw away his medicine while he was downstairs.'

'No way,' I said, but I felt myself blushing.

Vern and I watched Barry swallow his pills.

Vern himself swallowed four. As they went down he said, 'One–nil, two–nil, three–nil, four–nil. Woo-ee, that's better.'

Nobody said anything for a bit. Just the sound of the music. A band called Piltdown Git that my dad had produced. They sounded like chainsaws and bin lorries reversing. Everything—the room, Vern and Barry, the music—seemed suddenly far away and very near at the same time. I felt as if I had taken drugs, even though I had thrown the pills in the bin. I wondered if maybe the effects of the pills had seeped through the skin of my hands and into my bloodstream.

Vern giggled, breaking the silence. 'Hey, Mungo,' he said. 'Remember when that mental kid gobbed on you by the canal?'

'Yeah.' It was the first time we'd ever talked about the Gobber. In that split-second it all came back. The smell of him when I was in the headlock. His cheapo trainers. The way he just took it when I was hitting him, the way his face felt, soft-and-hard, on my knuckles. How my fist ached for days. How Mum thought

139

I was such a sweet innocent kid. How I could never be sure I hadn't killed the Gobber and for my whole life I would be waiting in case the doorbell rang and it was the cops:

*Are you Mungo McFall? Did you reside in Gloucester Crescent, Camden Town in the year 2006? A new way of detecting crime has been invented and we have now discovered that you were the killer of the asthmatic kid with special needs on the Regent's Canal all those years ago.*

I blushed again, feeling suddenly hot. Feeling pissed off with Vern, too, for poking away at all my weak and painful places.

'The look on your face with all that gob running down your hair,' said Vern. 'Eh, Monster?'

Barry said, 'Yeah. I've seen that bloke quite a bit round the Lock. He still gives out leaflets for that tattoo parlour. He's seen me but he doesn't know who I am.'

'You never told me that,' I said to Barry. 'You've seen the Gobber since that day? Is that right, Monster?'

'Yeah.'

I hadn't killed him! The Gobber was alive! Feeling a blip of relief and happiness I said, 'D'you still go and see the wolves in the park?'

Barry said, 'No.'

Vern said, 'We never went to see the wolves except when you wanted to. That was your weird shit.'

'You should do it. Look in their eyes. Their yellow

eyes are amazing. They're like those old marbles they sell at the Lock.'

Vern giggled and said, 'What are you on about, you mong? I think the drugs do work, my friend. Are you feeling it?'

'Definitely.' I made my voice sound sleepy. 'Hey. D'you remember my dad's creepers?'

'Yeah man,' said Vern. 'They were just ever so slightly cool.'

'D'you wanna see them?'


I went through to Mum's room, feeling much happier than I would have thought possible two hours before when we were returning from the failed attempt to find the Happy Valley. I was intending to bring Dad's famous shoes back to show the guys. But I couldn't find them. Resting on my knees, with one hand on the bed, I looked underneath, sweeping the torch around. In that dark, dusty square of space I saw some scrunched-up paper hankies, a nasal spray, a book, and a thin plastic box, but no crêpe-soled leopardskin creepers, UK size 10, as bought in the Doc Marten shop round the corner from Camden tube and as worn—almost non-stop until he had to go into hospital and Mum bought him horrible tartan slippers that he used to shuffle to the toilet in—by my father, the late Gerald, known as Gerry, McFall.

The door of Mum's room opened and Vern walked in. 'It's OK,' I said. 'I'll be back in a minute.' It felt wrong for him to be in Mum's room and I wanted him to get out.

One of Mum's bras was on the floor. Vern hooked it up with his right foot and mimed a powerful volley at the far wall. 'Fabregas. One–nil,' he said. The bra was stuck on his foot. He waggled his leg, trying to dislodge it, then bent down and pulled the bra off his toe. He held the bra up to his chest and started to jig about like a puppet.

Barry appeared at the door. 'Wass goin' on?' he said.

Vern said, 'Mung's a transvestite, didn't you know?'

Barry said, 'Are you?'

Vern said, 'So am I.'

Barry said, 'Really?'

'Course not, you complete div.'

'Do you mind?' I said. 'Just go back to my room and I'll bring the shoes through.'

'We prefer it here,' said Vern. 'Don't we, Monster?'

'Yeah,' said Barry.


The action had moved to Mum's room and there was nothing I could do to move it back. I looked at my watch. Depending on whether Mum decided to come home for lunch or have it in Bickleigh, she could be back any minute. 'Hey, guys,' I said. 'My mum'll be home soon and she's being a real fascist at the moment.'

'So?' said Vern. 'We'll hear her, won't we?'

Vern knew it bothered me, which was why he was making a thing of it. Typical Vern. I decided not to mention it any more and hope they got bored and went back to the music in my bedroom. Meanwhile I carried on looking for the creepers. After doing another sweep of the under-bed area, I turned my attention to the chest of drawers, pulling out knickers and bras, cardigans and pedal pushers and hair clips. But no creepers.

I had this sudden, horrible feeling Mum had chucked them. Panic, but trying not to show it. Maybe, when she said she was going to redecorate because she couldn't stand living with ghosts, Mum meant the ghost of Dad as well as of Grandma and Grandpa. I went back to the bed. I knew it was hopeless but part of me thought maybe, magically, the creepers would have re-appeared there. I hardly noticed that Vern was now wearing a pair of my mum's knickers on his head. This time I reached right under the bed and brought out each item to eliminate it from my search—the old paper hankies, the nasal spray, the book, called *Coping With Bereavement*, the thin plastic box. Same result.

Still with the knickers on his head, Vern was tripping around like a fairy with his arms held out. He thought he was being funny but he just looked pathetic. It annoyed me, that he was wearing Mum's underwear as a hat but I knew he was doing it to wind me up so I didn't say anything. I wondered if the drugs were affecting him or whether he was just pretending they were.

Barry started looking in the chest of drawers I'd already looked in. He pulled out a photo of my dad, from before I was born. He was on a beach in winter, wearing a long, what they called Afghan, coat, smiling and smoking. 'Who's that?' Barry said.

'Who do you think?' I said. 'Put it back. I've already looked there.'

Barry shrugged, replaced the photo in the drawer and looked at his watch. If there'd been any stones in Mum's bedroom, he'd have toe-poked one.

The cupboard was my last chance. To get there I had to wade through stuff from the chest of drawers that I'd left on the floor. I'd tidy it up later. I got down on my knees and brought out more stuff to add to it: a duvet, a computer stand, a lampshade, a hairdryer, an old teddy that belonged to Mum when she had plaits, a pair of flip-flops, a pair of beach jellies, a blue bottle of aftersun lotion that was leaking and sticky, the handbag Mum had had with her on the day we scattered Dad's ashes, Dad's creepers . . .

Dad's creepers were under the handbag.

'Got 'em,' I said, but even as I was saying it I was starting to feel angry and sad at what had happpened to one of them since I'd seen them last. I carried on standing there with my back to the room.

'Come on then, let's have a look,' said Barry.

'*Blu-blu, leopardskin shoes*,' sang Vern, jigging about.

'Forget it,' I said. 'It was a stupid idea anyway.'

'Ah, come on,' said Barry. He stood next to me and

looked down at the bottom of the cupboard. 'Pass 'em here, dude,' he said.

I shrugged and handed Barry the shoes. He cleared a space in the middle of the room, toe-poking aside the clothes and other stuff, and put the shoes in the space. Vern got down on his knees and worshipped the shoes, waving his hands towards them like we did to Thierry Henry. I didn't say anything. I couldn't work out whether he was taking the piss or he genuinely thought they were cool.

Besides, neither Vern nor Barry seemed to have noticed the obvious thing, the thing that hit me between the eyes and made my stomach feel queasy: one of the shoes had been ruined. Since the last time I saw the creepers, four days before, aftersun lotion had leaked over the left one and stained the leopard-skin with a horrible splodge of grey.

I tried to rub it off with a paper hanky but made it worse, made wide grey streaks and little bobbles of torn hanky on the yellow and black. I concentrated instead on an old tube ticket I'd found in the right creeper. It had been bought at Covent Garden on 7 April 2004 and cost £1.30 so Mum hadn't been going far. Or maybe it had been Dad's and he had bought the ticket while wearing his creepers. I pictured him standing at the ticket machine, fiddling around for money, while passers-by took sideways looks at his dazzling, ultra-cool feet.

If I was in my own little world at that point, so were Vern and Barry. They'd quickly lost interest in the shoes and were now over by Mum's bed, giggling and whispering. I just wished they'd get bored and go back to the bedroom so I could be on my own with the ruined creeper, but I knew that was the last thing they would do if I suggested it.

So I just got on with it. I put the ticket in my pocket, got Mum's hairbrush from the top of the chest of drawers and tried to brush away the double-damage to the left creeper caused by the aftersun lotion and my initial rubbing. But this didn't work either, it just spread the grey streaks. I brushed harder. Now the grey streaks started to join up. Harder and harder. The grey streaks merged. I stopped brushing. Right across the toe, the leopardskin had disappeared. It looked more like ratskin.

I did what you'd do with a rat. I threw the creeper hard at the wall. It hit the corner of a framed watercolour that Grandma had done, a typical manure munching scene of a thatched cottage and a stream. The picture fell, the glass smashed.

I threw myself face-down onto Mum's bed.

Silence, then suppressed giggles. Vern and Barry were laughing at me. Vern said, between giggles, 'Hey, Mung, cool it, yeah? It's just the drugs. It's just, like, *shoes*, know what I mean?'

I turned over and sat up. Vern still had the knickers on his head. He'd also put the bra on over his T-shirt. The empty frilly bra cups looked ridiculous. 'You haven't got a clue, have you?' I said.

'What?' Vern said, appealing to Barry. 'I'm just trying to smooth things, yeah?'

'Yeah well,' I said. I was already feeling ashamed for losing it and throwing the creeper at the wall. I imagined Vern and Barry discussing the incident on the train back to London and using it as evidence that I'd changed. I'd become a deranged manure muncher who they never wanted to see again. They were probably right. I just wanted this miserable day to end. But it was about to get worse. Much worse.

Vern said, 'Hey, Mung, guess what we found?' Vern was trying to cheer me up, he had that tone in his voice. I didn't reply and he said, 'All right, when does the F in UFO not stand for Flying?'

I still didn't reply. Then he whacked me on the ear with something cold and rubbery.

'Oi,' I said.

I couldn't work it out at first. In one hand Vern was holding the thin black plastic box I'd seen under Mum's bed. The box was open and empty and its contents were in Vern's other hand: a rubber disc with a thick edge. Vern waved it in front of my face. It was like a spaceship, a frisbee, a jellyfish. It was the off-white colour of doctors' rubber gloves that they shove up your bum. And that's what it smelt like (not of bums but of hospitals and antiseptic).

I took it by its edge and wobbled it about, looking at it. I was so dense I didn't twig straight away, I just had a feeling about it. It was the same feeling I had had with Dad when I was about six and he took me to this old-fashioned barber's in Tufnell Park.

The barber pumped the seat right up until I was staring at all this stuff arranged around the mirror in front of me. An old Arsenal team photo from before I was born. Postcards of topless women. Little packs of stuff called Durex. Durex! Somehow I knew that whatever it was, Durex was rude, and I shouldn't ask questions about it. But I asked anyway. The barber laughed and said, 'Over to you, Dad.'

Dad spoke in a mock-old-fashioned voice. 'Durex, my boy, is a useful adjunct to weekend activities. Isn't that right, barber?'

The barber joined in the joke. 'It is indeed, sir.' And he winked at me in the mirror.

Outside the shop I said, 'But what *is* Durex though?'

'It's rubber johnnies. Know what they are?'

And I said, 'Yes,' because I had vaguely heard of them.

Dad rubbed my bristly head and laughed. 'Good lad.'

The flying saucer/jellyfish was to do with sex.

Vern and Barry were giggling. Vern poked the centre of the rubber disc with his index finger and said, 'You EFF oh, geddit?'

And then I remembered the stuff handed round class that we had had such a laugh about. The condoms, wrapped and unwrapped, the silver-foil sheets of contraceptive pills, the rubber disc that we'd chucked around and made flying saucer jokes about that was known as a Dutch cap. It didn't seem so funny now.

Mum's contraceptive device. Wooaah. I handed it back to Vern and said, 'Put it back where you found it.'

'It was under the bed for quick access,' said Barry, and giggled.

'You are so thick, Monster,' I said.

'All right, cool it,' said Vern. He replaced the jelly-fish in the box, snapped the lid closed and slid it under the bed.

(My head was spinning with the implications and possibilities of Mum's jellyfish.)

Now Vern was being peacemaker and I realized I did like him sometimes, that I would miss him if I stopped seeing him. Which made me more depressed, because after today he definitely wouldn't want to see *me* again. He said to Barry, 'Mung's just having a bad drug thing. It goes that way sometimes. He'll get over it. How are you doin'? Are you feelin' the lift?'

(I couldn't work it out. I was pretty sure that the last time I had looked under the bed, four days before, the thin plastic box hadn't been there. Which meant—)

'A bit,' said Barry, but he didn't sound convincing.

Vern took the bottle of drugs from his pocket and shook it in front of Barry's face: *shuh shuh shuh.* 'Have some more,' he said.

Barry steppped back and said, 'Nuh.'

'OK OK.' Vern put the jar of pills on the bed, took the knickers off his head and draped them on Barry's. 'Have some knickers then. And the bra. Here you go. Put it it on properly. Got any Elvis, Mung? Got *Blue Suede Shoes?*'

(Was the jellyfish new? Had Mum just bought it? It seemed incredible that you could buy such things in Bickleigh, but maybe you could. Thai aubergines? You must be joking. Contraceptive devices? Barnsful.) 'What?' I said. 'I think so. On a compilation.'

'Right. You put your old man's shoes on, Mung, and I'll go and put the Elvis on in your room and we have a bit of a dance, yeah?'

And this reminded me of another reason I would miss Vern: that he made you do things that were so stupid they were a laugh. I told Vern where to find the Elvis CD and he went through from Mum's room to mine via the bathroom leaving all the doors open in between. I picked up Dad's shoes and placed them on the floor by the bed. The ruined one didn't look quite so ruined, now my spit had dried. I dangled my feet over the creepers, realizing that I'd never worn them before. Was it sacrilege to wear them, or would Dad think it was a laugh too? There was no doubt about that: a laugh.

I plunged my feet into the creepers. They were much too big. My feet slipped around inside them. The leather insides were cool and dry. Soothing. I closed my eyes. Wearing my dad's creepers reminded me of swimming in the Caribbean.

I tied the laces. In my bedroom, Elvis started to sing.

*It's one for the money*
*Two for the show*
*Three to get ready*
*Now go cat go*

I picked up the bottle of drugs and shook it in time to the music, then threw it at Barry. 'Come on,' I said, and Barry started to jig about half-heartedly while shaking the bottle.

*Do anything that you want to do, but uh-uh*
*Honey lay off my shoes*

I kept my eyes closed as I danced and sang. I wasn't dancing and singing because I was happy. I was doing it to stop myself thinking.

And then I opened my eyes and Mum was standing there.

# Chapter 12

Elvis carried on singing regardless. Mum shouted in the direction of my bedroom, 'Off, turn that off. Off. OFF,' until Vern must have heard and the music stopped. Then she stared at my feet, my feet in Dad's creepers. I stared at them myself. They weren't moving now. They looked like clown's feet. 'How dare you,' she said.

'How dare I what?' It was a genuine question.

She shook her head and moved her lips but no words came out. Then words did come out: 'You know very well, Mungo. Making—making merry with your father's things.'

'But,' I said, 'I—' I couldn't believe what she was saying, what she was accusing me of. It was the opposite of the truth.

As I stepped out of the creepers, Mum turned her stare on Barry, who had her underwear all over him and looked like a pervert. Barry put the bottle of Vern's drugs he'd been shaking on the edge of the bed, then stared at the carpet, but did not remove the knickers and bra he was wearing. If I hadn't been so freaked out this would have been quite funny, because he was being even more of a div than Vern and I pretended he was. Mum picked up the bottle, looked at the label and said, 'I didn't know you were menopausal already, Barry.'

Barry said, 'Eh?'

Mum shook her head and stared at Monster, who continued to stare at the carpet while wearing her underwear. 'At least have the decency,' she said.

Barry looked up with his mouth open but still did not do or say anything. I whispered to him, 'Take the stuff off, you div.'

Barry said, 'Oh, right,' and then had a job getting his arms out of the bra straps. Mum folded her arms and looked out of the window, tapping her foot and clutching Vern's drugs tightly in her right hand, while Barry got himself disentangled. He laid the bra and knickers on the bed very carefully, as if they were precious, breakable objects.

'God help us,' said Mum to herself. To us she said: 'Right. Downstairs. Now.' Then, remembering someone was missing, she said, 'Trust Vernon to be the only sensible one.' I just stared at her. Double disbelief. Mum went through to the bathroom and called through the open door to my bedroom. 'You too, Vernon. Downstairs now.'

Mum placed the bottle of Vern's drugs in the middle of the kitchen table, then got warmed up by giving Barry a major bollocking. 'How dare you, how dare you,' she said, prodding him on the shoulder, 'bring your uncouth ways down here? What did these people ever do to you, to merit such cheek?'

We looked at each other. What was she going on about? I said, 'What?'

She turned to me. 'You know what, Mungo. You put him up to it. With all your patronizing rubbish about manure eaters. What makes you think you're so superior?'

'Munchers,' I said. Then it clicked. Mum had talked to the Bozo and he had sneaked about Vern giving him the finger when he drove past in the bozomobile. Except Mum assumed it was Barry who'd done it because she was biased against Barry. 'What a creep,' I said. 'The Bozo's been sneaking on us.'

'He was shaken by it, if you want to know. People aren't used to this kind of gratuitous aggression down here. And then'—Mum banged her forehead with the soft bit of her thumb—'blow me, but half an hour later it happens again on the main road. For your information, Barry, you only gave the finger to an off-duty policeman, that's all.'

We giggled because she'd said 'gave the finger'.

I said, 'How d'you know about *that*?'

'Because this is a close-knit community where people still talk to each other. But you wouldn't know about that.'

I said, 'It's a horrible place where everybody knows everybody else's business and they try and make you do what you don't want to do. And anyway, you're

154

completely wrong about Barry. It wasn't Barry. That's just you being biased because Barry hasn't got a dad and his mum works for Camden Council. Well guess what, I haven't got a dad either, and my mum works in a charity shop for about ten quid a day selling shit to dead people. Not only that. She . . . she—' I was going to mention Mum's Dutch cap. But I didn't, I couldn't, it was too messed up in my head. The moment passed and I knew it was too late.

I didn't realize till I stopped that I'd been shouting. Mum was staring at me. Vern and Barry were staring at the floor. I wanted Vern to own up to what he'd done, to say that it was him, not Barry, who had given the finger to those cars. But I knew he wouldn't.

Mum said to me, 'So it was you, was it? Well, at least you have the decency to admit it.'

'Oh, bollocks, forget it,' I said.

Mum laughed through tight lips and said, 'Believe me, I haven't even got started yet.'

She went on and on about what she'd caught us doing in the bedroom, how dancing to Elvis while wearing knickers on your head wasn't remotely funny or clever, it was delinquent and disturbed behaviour and she was going to have to report it to Vern's and Monster's mums, for their own good, of course (yeah yeah). Then she picked up the bottle of Vern's drugs from the table and stared at us one by one. 'Who'd like to go first?' she said. 'Who'd like to have a go at explaining this one away? Mungo?'

I shrugged.

'Barry? You brought this with you, I take it.'

Monster said, 'No,' but it didn't sound convincing because he was the sort of div who feels guilty even when he's innocent.

'I see,' Mum said.

She wasn't even going to ask Vern. She reckoned she'd already found the guilty one and that made me suddenly angry, so angry I just came out with it.

'No, you don't see,' I said. 'You don't see anything. Vern brought those, all right? They're Vern's drugs. He nicked them off his mum. I didn't even have any.'

Mum stared at me then turned her head and stared at Vern. Vern stared at *me*, and I looked at the floor. 'Is this right, Vernon?' Mum said.

And for the first time Vern didn't bother being all creepily nice to my mum. He just said, 'Whatever,' in a real Camden way, and I knew he hadn't even glanced at Mum, that all the time he was staring at the top of my head as I looked at the floor, willing all this horrible shit into my head with his laser-beam eyes.

Guess what, I never saw Vern again after that moment that I sneaked on him. I saw Barry once more, which you'll hear about soon enough.

Mum banned them from coming down again, and me from going up to Camden to see them, then she took them to the station and I stayed behind in the cottage and used the time to start activating Plan A, by filling my backpack with a few things I might need for the next part of my life. When Mum got back from the station she rang Vern's and Barry's mums and told them everything including about the drugs, then she called me down to the kitchen.

She was holding the bottle of drugs again. She'd told Vern's mum on the phone that she was hanging on to them for safekeeping. 'Do you know what these are?' she said. 'What does it say on the bottle?'

'I dunno.'

'Take it. Read it.'

I took the jar and read the label. I'd never seen the word. I didn't know how to pronounce it. 'Deepo, pro, something.' I shrugged and put the bottle back on the table.

Mum said, 'Depo-Provera is a brand name for something called progesterone. Do you know what progesterone is? It's a hormone they give to women during the menopause. Do you know what the menopause is?'

'Sort of.'

'What is the menopause?'

'It's something to do with eggs.' I giggled. 'So what'll happen to Vern? Will he have a baby?'

Mum smashed her fist down on the table. 'This is not funny, Mungo,' she shouted. 'You think you're so clever. You think you know so much. And you don't know diddle-squat.'

'The word is diddly-squat.' It was one of Dad's words. I thought of the half-filled backpack upstairs, and waited for Mum to come back at me. We didn't have rows when Dad was around, not like this. My wolf was here beside me, and I reckoned Mum had an invisible wolf too, right beside her. There were no wolves in the house when Dad was alive. The only wild animals were the ones they covered the toes of his leopardskin creepers in, and that wasn't real leopardskin. Nothing was harmed in the making of Dad's shoes except for a cow which they were killing anyway, so people could eat it. But the world was different now.

Mum stared into my eyes. She said, 'I'm not rising to your bait.'

'Dad would have thought it was funny,' I said. 'The next time he saw Vern he'd have said, "Bump not showing yet then, Vernon?"'

I knew what I said was true. I stared back into Mum's eyes, willing her to admit it. She said, 'Let's get one thing straight, once and for all. Your father is dead. Nothing's going to change that. You can be as angry and destructive as you like. You can insult me and lie to me and embarrass me, but your dad is not coming back. Do you understand?'

I stood up. 'You're doing my head in,' I said. 'I'm going to play some music.'

Mum smashed the table with the flat of her hand and shouted, 'Siddown. You still don't understand, do you? Well, let me spell it out for you. You will learn to adjust to life down here. Seeing that you are congenitally incapable of being civil to Brian, you will have a chat with a policeman friend of ours who will put you straight on a few things. You will see Talullah Boland—'

I shouted, 'No fucking way.'

I couldn't believe it. Mum slapped me. The same hand that smashed down on the table reached out and whipped across my face. My cheek felt hot as a light-bulb. I ran up to my room.

I lay on my bed and watched the sky darken through the window. Birds were singing like nutcases: happy songs that said Welcome to Manuresville. It wasn't their fault. They didn't know something terrible had happened.

I tried to concentrate on little things, so my mind wouldn't obsess about the big thing, which was the question of Mum's jellyfish and what it meant, which was another way of saying—But I stopped the thought, and had another, less dangerous one instead: who was this copper she was on about? Dad didn't like coppers, he wouldn't have one in the house. He certainly wouldn't have one in to lecture me on how to behave. My cheek still stung.

Downstairs, the telephone pinged. She'd probably been yabbering to Barbara. I bet the wine was open and the bottle already half-empty. I heard the kitchen door open. Mum walked through the summer room and came halfway up the stairs. Silence, then she said, 'Mungo?' Her voice sounded surprisingly close.

I didn't say anything.

'Would you like some pizza?'

'No.'

'You've got to eat.'

I didn't say anything.

Mum carried on up the stairs. She was outside the door. 'I shouldn't have slapped you. I'm sorry.'

I didn't say anything.

'Can I come in?'

'No. I'm asleep.'

I watched the door handle, waiting for it to turn, waiting for Mum to come in. But it didn't turn, and then Mum went back down the stairs.

I wished I'd said yes to the pizza.


The thoughts came back in the night, and this time I couldn't stop them. My mind was like a beach and the thoughts were like big angry waves, wave after wave, crashing on it.

My mum was having sex. Or planning to. There could be only one person she was having sex with, or planning to.

Wooaa. Don't go there.

But I had to go there. The Bozo.

Mum was shagging the Bozo. Or wanting to.

Mum had kicked out the creepers and moved in the jellyfish. She didn't even know or care that a load of aftersun had stained the left creeper. She was too busy thinking of putting out for the Bozo. Or—another thought—maybe even actually putting out for the Bozo, already. When I was out on my bike, for instance, he might come round and they might do it. Already they might be doing it. And another bad thought: was the jellyfish new or old? Was it the one she used to use with Dad, or had she gone out and bought a new one especially for the Bozo? And which would be worse?

These thoughts were bad enough. But then the biggest waves of all landed, more like tsunamis than waves. A fragment of the nightmare I'd had down the well came back to me: the feeling that the Bozo was my dad and there was nothing I could do about it. Maybe, I thought, Mum had been putting out for years, before I was born and after. Maybe, as a result, the Bozo really was my dad—tsunami number one.

And here was tsunami number two, following quickly behind: maybe I had a secret bastard brother, and this secret bastard brother had a name: Mungo, for instance. Obvious, really—he was a slimehead like me, and how else would he know all that stuff about my great-grandfather?

Don't go there. Or, go on, shoot me in the head.

When this double-tsunami landed my first impulse was to activate Plan A immediately. There and then, whatever time it was, i.e. four o'clock in the morning. But then I imagined a wolf stepping out into the road in front of me and its yellow eyes flashing a warning, telling me to be calm, to think it through. I had no money. I'd be found within a few hours and have to come back to the cottage with no ammunition left. Plus, knowing my luck, the Bozo would be the one who found me, which would make him even more of a hero in Mum's eyes.

No, I had to do the calm and canny wolf thing. I had to play the game with Mum, which meant going along with the ridiculous PC Manurehead idea. I had to smile at Mum and offer to help her strip paint off the walls, and oh what a nice colour that would be for the summer room bullshit. And when I was ready I had to act. Quick and silent, like wolves.

This was the wolf decision that eventually calmed the waves, turned them into a flat sea, the Caribbean sea, on which I floated and slept.


When I woke in the morning the double tsunami hit me all over again. The Bozo was my real dad and the div otherwise known as Mungo was my secret bastard brother who'd been playing me along all the time. Mum too. She was part of the deceit, obviously. I couldn't even bring myself to look at her, but while she made me a bacon sarnie I tried to stay calm. When I'd finished eating it she spoke the first words she'd said to me since the previous evening at five o'clock. 'PC Strickland is coming round for a chat at twelve fifteen; he's kindly giving up his lunch break. I'll be back at twelve. Please tidy your room.'


The world was spinning. PC Manurehead's face was going round and round me. It was a yellow and red face with a ginger moustache. Below the moustache, his lips were very red and very shiny, like internal organs that shouldn't really be on show. Words were coming out of his mouth. If his words had been visible, they would have looked like the Gobber's gob mixed with the Smelly Man's toe cheese.

I watched his face like you watch a merry-go-round at a fair. Dad took me to a fair once on Hampstead Heath. He was chuffed because the bloke operating the waltzers was wearing leopardskin creepers.

I imagined PC Manurehead combing his moustache every morning in front of the bathroom mirror. He got his big red-and-yellow face very close to the mirror so he could comb it very neatly.

Behind PC Manurehead's head, the kitchen was also spinning. I kept seeing the mug tree passing by, the trees outside the window. Mum was upstairs in her bedroom. I heard her moving about. Maybe she was checking on the whereabouts of the jellyfish. The landing creaked. Mum had gone into the bathroom. She was giving us enough time to have a proper bond. PC Manurehead would give me a lecture about life as it is lived in the Bickleighs of this world, and I would be very grateful and change in the space of twenty-five minutes from a wayward and deceitful delinquent into a well-balanced young man with a surprisingly mature outlook on life and a desire to play with Talullah Boland. Not.

Here are some of the words that came out of Manurehead's mouth and would have looked like a cross between gob and toe cheese if you could have seen them as they went splatting around the kitchen:

sense of belonging
**considerate behaviour**
birdwatching, *strictly* of the feathered variety I
  might add *hee hee*
**volunteering** for the village litter patrol

down
  on
  you
    like a
    **TON OF BRICKS**

life's *not* a rehearsal
you could *do worse*
than consider joining the very
**active** scout troop we have here in the village.

When Manurehead closed his mouth and the words
stopped spewing out, I smiled and said, 'Thank you very
much, PC Strickland. I'll bear that in mind. And thanks for
taking the time to come and see me.' My voice sounded as
if it was coming from the far end of a long dark tunnel.

After Manurehead had effed off, I smiled at Mum
too and said that Manurehead—I called him PC
Strickland—had said some very interesting things that I
would definitely be taking on board and I thanked her for
asking him over. Then I said I would take the pictures
down in the summer room, and stack the furniture, and

164

scrub down the walls ready for painting. And Mum frowned, suddenly Smelling a Rat, and I knew I'd gone too far. So I laughed and said, All right then, I might go out on my bike instead, and Mum ruffled my hair and smiled back at me and said she was going back to the charity shop for the afternoon. And I thought, I wonder if that's where you're really going. When she hugged me goodbye, I had to make a real effort to give her a proper squeeze back because I was thinking of her hugging the Bozo.

Mum thought the war was over but it hadn't even begun.

When she'd gone I waited the usual ten minutes in case she came back because she'd forgotten something. Then I went up to her bedroom to see if she'd taken the jellyfish with her. The jellyfish was still under the bed. I hesitated but decided to leave it where it was. I opened the wardrobe door and checked the pockets of her coats and jackets. I found a two-pound coin, two one pound coins, and some other coins that all together came to five pounds seventy-one. But the real money was downstairs. In the jar marked COOKIES were two twenty pound notes. I took them. I also took an unopened packet of six muesli bars, an opened packet of cheese, two bags of cheese and onion crisps, and a carton of Ribena. All this went in my backpack along with the fleece and Grandpa's binoculars and Swiss Army knife that I'd packed the night before.

I put my backpack on and biked off for Bickleigh station. Plan A was up and running.

# Chapter 13

On my way to the station it started to rain. Looking back, I should have picked up the clue earlier. It was always raining when I met Mungo. The rain made him appear from nowhere like the frogs and the earthworms. And when it stopped raining, he did his vanishing act. He told me later, in that weird boffinish way he had, that us meeting up was to do with the sudden drop in barometric pressure. But I was a million miles from sussing anything like that out that afternoon.

So it started to rain and then I saw Mungo. My bike whooshed round a corner in the lane and there he was, up on the bank, mucking about at the edge of the pond. The pond level was so high it was spilling over the bank and forming a mini waterfall that gurgled into the lane and ran downhill in a twisting torrent of white water. I didn't intend to stop—he was the last person I wanted to see or talk to. But as I slowed down to steer through the rushing pond water Mungo leapt from the bank and stood in front of my front wheel.

'What do you want?' I said. 'Get out of the way.'

'I'm trying to dam the pond, and generally checking for newts,' he said, 'if you want to help me.' He looked desperate and his face, in all that rain and gloom, was like a Camden Town goth's: the jet-black hair, the white face, the startled look.

'I know who you are,' I said. 'And I never want to see you again. I never want to see any of you again. Tell Mum I know who my real dad is and I'm leaving for ever. Now shift your arse.'

But Mungo wouldn't get out of the way. 'Who am I then?'

'You're a bastard and I wish you were dead,' I said, 'and you can tell Mum that from me.'

'No no no, you don't understand,' he said. 'Have you read the book? You must read it. It's all in there.'

'I know all about the book. You're not going to get me that way. Now just piss off out of it. I've had enough of this.'

'What does the book say then?'

I rammed my front wheel into the top of Mungo's thigh and mimed jerking the handlebars round, meaning: next time I'll get you where it *really* hurts. 'Shift,' I said. 'Now.'

Mungo's face crumpled. He hung his head, and when he looked back up white snot was bubbling at his nostrils. He was crying. 'I know it's a mess,' he said. 'You should never do things because you're sad, I know that now. I just want you to understand.'

Mungo was like a horrible disease that was almost impossible to get rid of. Whatever you did or said, he found something else to come back at you with—like bullshitting about being sad and crying so much that his nose bubbled with snot. But this time I had the cure. I was never going to see him again.

'Yeah yeah, get a life,' I said, 'preferably a million miles away from me.' And I steered the front wheel round him and whooshed off through the rain.

Where does London start?

It was still raining. Blobs of rain were vibrating along the train window. I was looking at fields with cows in them, all huddled along the hedges against the rain. Then my eyelids closed and Dad was in the carriage, sitting across from me and looking at me sideways. He was grinning. He said, 'What deep shit is this you've got yourself into?'

And I said, 'Hey, Dad, hi.' I couldn't give him all the details, they would have upset him, so I just said, 'The sort of deep shit that only you can get me out of.'

The bloke opposite me's mobile went off. The ringtone sounded like a lion belching. I opened my eyes. Outside the window, the fields and cows had gone. There were cranes, and filthy brick, and spraycanned bits of twisted metal that were sculptures that were supposed to make Londoners feel better about their environment that was covered in spraycanned brick and metal. There were bridges covered in multicoloured spraycanned tags, and tower blocks covered in satellite dishes. In my head Dad jigged up and down and said, 'I hate trees, I hate fresh air and I particularly have it in for blinking bluebells. Gimme tattoo parlours and satellite dishes and filthy old brick any day of the week. Yeah!'

After Clapham Junction the train driver said, 'This is the South-West Trains service to London Waterloo only.' We went past Battersea Power Station, which I recognized from one of Dad's Pink Floyd albums. I didn't know this part of London but it still felt like home. It was like when I met Dad's brother Jack, who I hadn't met before because he lived in Toronto, at Dad's funeral. I didn't know him and knew him at the same time. When he met me he punched my arm and hugged me. He didn't say anything, not straight away. He didn't have to.

That gave me an idea. Maybe I could move to Toronto and live with Uncle Jack.

I saw the Darth Vader noses of the Eurostar trains all lined up in their long glass shed, then the driver said, 'This is London Waterloo. The train terminates here. All change, please. Please take care when leaving the train and ensure you have all your belongings with you.'

I stood up. The train lurched and I almost fell over. I swung my backpack up with one arm and went to stand by the door. The train stopped, the doors hissed. I pressed the big squishy button, and the doors slid open. I stepped into London and all its weird heavy air that was like a bath.

I closed my eyes and lay down in the bath right up to my chin. I couldn't imagine being anywhere else.

* * *

The world was spinning, I could feel it. I could have been a million billion other people, if you count the whole of history, but I was me, right now, whizzing under London on the Northern Line quite near the beginning of the twenty-first century. Somebody was getting off the train and I was taking their place on a flip-up seat. Opposite me sat a black girl wearing a T-shirt that said, 'Funky cool ultra kinky'. I could have been her just as easily as I was in fact me. I imagined being her looking at me, wondering who I was and what I was doing. She would never guess in a million years I was running away because my dad wasn't my real dad and my mum had a bastard son who was my secret brother. But she wasn't looking at me anyway, she was checking her mobile. Maybe she never wondered who she could have been instead of herself.

Some old Japanese people were spread about the carriage. I noticed them blinking at each other, saying things with blinks the way Mum and I communicated with eyes and eyebrows. *Used* to communicate—I wasn't planning to see Mum ever again. I started to wonder why Mungo had been crying, and what he had meant when he said that stuff about being sad. But I forced myself to stop thinking about him in case I started to feel sorry for him.

The Japs got off at Tottenham Court Road.

* * *

From Hampstead tube I walked up the hill past a shop selling crap sculptures of naked women and another shop selling big oil paintings of American diners and gas stations from before Dad was even born. Dad would have hated the naked women and loved the gas stations. Then there was a Thai restaurant with two huge golden buddhas in the window and I half-thought of going in and asking if they had any Thai aubergines but there wasn't any point because I wasn't ever going back to Manure Munching Land, and Mum would never again deserve to have a special surprise meal cooked by me with candles burning and Elvis Costello on the sound system.

This was the way we came on the day of the ashes-scattering. There was Mum and me and Jack and three of Dad's mates from when he was a student and lived at Gospel Oak and they flew kites on Parliament Hill, and Barbara and Barbara's husband Col, who was an engineer in Formula One and I expected him to turn up in a really flash car but it was just a Volvo. We walked in a crocodile up the hill. Dad's mates were first, then Mum, then me, then Jack with a small back-pack in one hand and Dad in a plastic urn in an Oddbins bag in the other, which everyone thought was quite funny, then Barbara and Col. We didn't dress up, not like for the funeral. Mum said not to. She said it was just a walk with old friends, with an added point to it. It was a sunny day, which seemed inappropriate, like when the birds sang Welcome to Manuresville at the wrong moment. It was also windy. I was worried about that wind, about what it would do to the ashes.

People walked past us and didn't know what we were doing. They didn't know that the bloke in the jeans and grey jacket was carrying his brother in a bag, that his brother who was my dad had recently been put in an oven at the temperature of the earth's core and burnt till he didn't exist except as grey powder. That we were all going to stand on top of a hill and release Dad till he didn't exist at all, not even as grey powder.

But then again I didn't know what the people who walked past us were doing. They might have just killed an injured pigeon with a brick. I saw someone do that on the Regent's Canal towpath. His face had no expression. You couldn't tell whether he did it because he was kind or because he was cruel and it was a good excuse.

Walking across the Heath, Uncle Jack said to me, 'I bet you didn't know your dad was a champion sprinter when he was at school.'

It was true, I didn't know. I said, 'Really?'

'Absolutely true. Middlesex Schools one hundred and two hundred metre champion nineteen seventy-eight. He had trials for the national squad.'

I tried to imagine Dad in running gear, but I couldn't do it. I just kept seeing him in his leather waistcoat and his creepers.

\* \* \*

I was trying to remember the direction we had walked across the Heath. Just when I thought I was lost I saw the Two-Dimensional Tree. We had walked past it on the day of the ashes-scattering. It was a big tree with a thick trunk, on the top of a hill. When Mum and Dad and I used to walk on the Heath on Sundays we always commented on that tree because the way it was silhouetted against the sky made the trunk look flat. Dad called it the Two-Dimensional Tree. When we walked past it on the day of the ashes-scattering I really hoped Mum wouldn't tell the story. It was a secret story just between her and me, now that Dad wasn't here. And she didn't say anything, but she turned and smiled at me, to show she'd seen it.

A fine drizzle started to fall. I wasn't sure exactly where Parliament Hill was but I just sort of sensed the right direction. Dad said that seas and hills pull you to them, they have a sort of magnetism. And eventually I was zigzagging across springy grass and it was making the bottom of my jeans wet and rain was spraying in my face but I didn't care because the ground was widening out and sloping up and other people were walking into view from different directions, we were all doing the same thing, we were going to the top of Parly Hill.

Dad's idea wasn't to have his ashes scattered here, or not the way we did it that day. He wanted to be launched into the sky in a firework. He wanted his ashes put in the nose-cone of a rocket. We'd all go to

Parly Hill and do a countdown, then light the fuse and watch him go. He told Mum this years ago, when he was healthy and expected to live to ninety. It was in Barbados and I was there when he said it, sitting outside a jazz café in Bridgetown with a musician with gold teeth. Dad winked at me when he said it, and the musician laughed so much you could count his teeth. I reminded Mum after he died but she wouldn't do it. She said he hadn't meant it but I reckoned it was a typical Dad idea. But I didn't argue. Mum seemed strong then. You didn't argue with her.

But she wasn't really strong after all, she was a betrayer. It shocked me, to suddenly think of Mum and the Bozo as I walked up the side of Parly Hill. The tsunami again. My dad wasn't my dad! My dad wasn't my dad!

Oh yes he was. This was my dad's time and my dad's day, whatever new information I had. I pushed Mum, Mungo, and the Bozo into a hole in the hill and kicked soil over them until their memories stopped breathing.

The bench I was looking for, right on top of the hill, was empty. On the back of the bench had been carved, 'In Loving Memory of Martha A. Tomlin'. I sat on it and got a muesli bar out, and as I munched it I looked out on the opposite of Manuresville. London.

The rain and cloud made for poor visibility. The greatest city on earth looked like shit. Its buildings were spread out like a long table after a heavy party, the sort of party we used to have in Gloucester Crescent when one of Dad's albums was coming out and Mum had to ask Dad to make sure that the taking of illicit substances was confined to his studio room on the first floor, in case Plod paid a visit. They never did, and I never did manage to get into Dad's studio on those nights, but I used to hang around downstairs; I saw what can happen to tables. And London looked like a trashed party table, strewn with plastic plates and half-gnawed chicken drumsticks and scrunched beer cans. It was silent. All those millions of people down there, the taxis and vans and motorbike couriers and trains. And it was silent as the middle of the night, three hours after the last person's left the party.

Once, when Dad was flying his kite up here when he was a student, he met Fergal Shearkey of the Undertones and had a chat with him. Ten years later, Dad met Fergal in a studio and reminded him they'd once met on the top of Parly Hill but Fergal didn't remember.

Mum and Dad and I came up here in 1999 to watch the eclipse of the sun. There were hundreds of people, hundreds of kids, all wearing these special protective specs that were given away by a newspaper, including me. It was before school, eight o'clock in the morning. We waited and waited but the sky seemed to darken only a tiny bit, and I was disappointed. But Dad said, 'Look at the swallows.' These fast birds with forked tails were twisting and swooping all over the top and edge of the hill. 'They're catching insects. The insects start flying because it's got dark so they think it's evening. And the swallows also think it's evening because the insects are flying. Isn't that amazing?'

Then Dad gave me a lecture, just about the only one he ever gave me because in general he wasn't the sort of Dad who gives lectures. It was about how things don't have to be spectacular to be amazing. 'Stadium rock is spectacular but not amazing. A swallow thinking it's evening at eight o'clock in the morning is amazing but not spectacular. Comprendee?'

On that ashes-scattering day, Jack had a problem with the urn. Mum and him and I sat on the Martha A. Tomlin bench and the rest stood around, pretending to look out at London. Their hair was being blown back by the wind. Dad's old Gospel Oak mates turned round to light fags, then faced out again at the silent city. They were pretending to look at the millions of invisible people down there because they didn't want to have to look at what Jack was doing. He was sorting the urn, or trying to.

He took it out of the Oddbins bag and put it on the bench between me and him, then changed his mind and moved it to the other side, between him and Mum, between his backpack and her handbag. Mum glanced at it but pretended to be more interested in St Paul's Cathedral. Jack whispered, 'Ready?' and Mum nodded her head slightly. The urn was made of plastic that was supposed to look like bronze but it just looked even more like plastic. It was like a big coffee jar, it had a screw top. The screw top was the problem. Jack couldn't unscrew it. I was watching him across Mum's body. First of all he tried a quick, casual twist. Then, when that didn't work, he tipped it over almost on its side to get a better grip and ended up pulling a face, he was twisting so hard. You imagined the top suddenly coming off and the contents—Dad—going all over the place. But still the top wouldn't budge. It was quite funny. I kept thinking there was someone I couldn't wait to tell this to, when it was all over. Then I realized that the 'someone' I meant, the person I wanted to tell more than anybody, was in the urn.

Eventually Jack called out, 'Here, Steve,' and Mum stood up from the bench and walked down the hill a bit while Gospel Oak Steve came over and managed to unscrew the top of the urn for Jack. I thought Mum might look at me, might be bothered about what I felt at this moment, with my dad trapped in a coffee jar, but she looked at her feet the whole time as if she was admiring how pointy the toes of her shoes were. Jack joined her and they stood together about ten metres down the hill for a few seconds, looking at the Houses of Parliament, looking at a communications mast on a hill on the far horizon that looked like a mirror image of Parly Hill but was in fact Crystal Palace because Dad told me.

Then Mum turned round and smiled at me and I went and joined her and she put her arm round me and the rest of the people followed and we stood in a semi-circle and Mum said, 'I was going to say a few words but I'm sure you all have your private thoughts about Gerry at this point so I think we should just stand in silence with our thoughts for a few seconds and then Jack will give Gerry his freedom. The—' And then Mum started crying, but she recovered very quickly and said: 'The freedom of the wind and the sky and the North London that he loved. Oh dear, I've said a few words after all.' And she snuffled and laughed and squeezed me, and I squeezed her back, and everybody laughed a bit and then we all stood not saying anything and I wasn't looking at London, the million buildings and people, I was looking at the red running track down at the bottom of the hill, I was looking at one person running round it, making no noise, not making a mark in all the redness. And then Mum whispered, 'OK, Jack,' and Jack unscrewed the top but didn't take it right off.

Instead he said, 'Um . . . I don't think—I mean, I think we need to turn round because—The wind. It'll—' And he didn't need to say any more. We turned round, we turned our backs on London, and Jack whistled off the top of the urn and Dad unravelled like a sudden scarf made of dust, a brief grey Milky Way of ash that vanished for ever across Parly Hill, all except the stuff that landed on Mum's handbag and Jack's backpack on the bench and that Jack tried to pat away discreetly as he swung the backpack on to his shoulder. Mum didn't pat away her ash. But afterwards that handbag went to the bottom of the cupboard, I did notice that.

There was no one on the running track today. I tilted my head back into the rain. I saw the raindrops falling in seeming slow motion, following them down till my eyes lost focus and the rain tickled my face. If Dad was up there, the raindrops should be grey with the Milky Wayness of my dad. But the drops looked clear. I wiped them from my forehead, my ears, and looked at my fingers. They were fresh and pink, not a trace of ash.

No one was near. I could talk quite loudly, which I usually did in the sound-proofed chamber of my head when other people were about. Talk to Dad, I mean. I remembered the brief conversation we had had on the train on the way up to Waterloo. I said out loud, 'Yeah, as you said, I am in deep shit. I won't go into it here cos you probably won't like all the details, but the point is, what do I have to do to get out?'

And I waited for Dad to answer, like he usually did. Wherever I was—in bed, at school, down a well—Dad would answer. I would make him answer.

Waiting for him to answer, I listened to the wind and rain and watched no one going round the red running track.

When Dad was dying he didn't say he was dying to me

179

or to Mum, and Mum didn't say he was dying to me or to Dad, and I didn't say he was dying to Mum or Dad or to myself. We just said he was going through a bit of a bugger. It was February and cold as hell. Mum made him lentil stew with onions and leeks and bits of chorizo in it and ordered some travel brochures and sat on the edge of his bed and they picked the villa we were going to stay in in Sicily when he got better. Dad's bed was in his downstairs study by then because it was easier for Mum to keep an eye on him while she was in the kitchen, and his study had its own loo. It also had his gold discs around the walls and a humungous sound system but he never played any music when he was in bed in that room. He wasn't interested in music by then, he wasn't interested in anything—not books or telly, or even what the weather was like. Except once.

Once I went in to see him and he was reading a book of poetry that Mum had bought him a few years ago and he'd never got round to looking at before. It was by a poet who'd once lived nearby at Primrose Hill and his wife had committed suicide there. Dad looked up from the pages when I went in and said, 'Now then, kidder.' Then he called Mum. 'Hey, Clare,' he said. 'Listen to this.' Mum appeared with a tea towel in her hand and leant in the doorway. Dad read a poem about a friend of the poet's called Lucas who had never changed in forty years and was like a stone on a riverbed. Then he looked up, over the top of the book and said, 'Guess who Lucas is?'

Mum shook her head. 'I don't—'

'Steve!'

He meant Gospel Oak Steve. Before Dad got ill he hadn't been in touch with Steve for years because Steve was a teacher and earned a lot less than Dad and Dad said the money thing got a bit awkward. But as soon as Dad got ill he came round all the time. Mum said he was one of life's good people.

Mum said, 'Oh, I see.'

'Don't you just love that? Like a stone on the bed of a river.'

'I thought you didn't like poetry?'

And for a split second, with them bantering, it was like it used to be.

Mum made mugs of tea when people came to visit him and answered questions for him when he was too tired to reply. She talked a lot, more than she usually did. It was as if her words were keeping the roof of the world propped up, and if her words stopped, the roof of the world would collapse.

But then one day the words did stop, and the roof of the world did cave in, and I knew. I was in the kitchen, eating cheese on toast. Mum was in with Dad and Steve. I could hear them laughing. Then there was silence. Then Mum came into the kitchen really quickly. She pushed the door closed behind her, and burst into tears. She'd made it in to the kitchen just in time, like when you nearly don't make it to the toilet.

She said to me, 'I'm sorry,' and shook her head, shook the tears out of her eyes. Then she stood in the corner, facing the rack of spice jars that I once helped her fill and label, a million years ago when Mum was a nice mum, not a tart with a secret son, and I was a nice kid and not a devious and violent adolescent. She didn't make a noise but I knew she was crying. I was going to get up and go to her. But she looked so rigid. I pictured myself walking over and putting my arm round her and it was like hugging a goalpost. She didn't want me, not then. She wanted Dad.

She wanted him coming up behind her, unshaven in leopardskin creepers with the day's first glass of wine on his breath. So I didn't go to her, I did the only thing I could think of to make her feel better. I crunched the crust of my cheese on toast extra loud. And I thought about the thing I knew, the thing I now knew I had known all along. Dad was dying.

After we threw his ashes to the sky and wind on Parliament Hill, Mum said to think of Dad as all around.

And I said, 'Will he always be all around?'

'If you want him to be, yes. But after a while—you may not think so now—but after a while, you won't want him to be quite so much. So he won't be. That's how it works. Time helps us.'

'Time kills him off, you mean.'

And now I thought, between seeing Dad on the train to Waterloo and getting to Parliament Hill—in those few minutes when I was rattling under London on the

182

Northern Line near the beginning of the twenty-first century—time had finally done what it always does. And Dad was dead.

From Parly Hill I walked down to Kentish Town tube. I bought a kebab on the way and ate it on the tube to Camden. At Camden I came up on the escalator into all that smell, of onions and fish sauce and weed and tramps, and kebab on my fingers.

I went out of the left-hand entrance and turned left. Two doors down was the Doc Marten shop. I looked for creepers like Dad's in the window but there weren't any. I went in. The same girl was there who sold Dad his creepers. I recognized her because she had a flower tattooed on her throat. She said, 'Are you looking for something in particular?' except she said 'partickla'.

I said, 'No,' and started looking round. I didn't see them at first. Then I spotted them. They were on the floor at the back. The left one was in the box and the right one was displayed on top of the box. I picked it up. On the sole, the crepe was clean as a baby's arse. The 'leopardskin' was nice and tufty, the creeper weighed just right, as much as a small melon. The girl was watching me. She said, 'Proper George Cox, them.'

'I know.' I almost asked her if she remembered me coming in with my dad when he bought his pair. Then I could tell her that my dad was dead. But I was sure she didn't remember.

When Dad had tried his on, she had said, 'They're the bees' knees, them.'

Dad had said, 'They are, aren't they?'

And she had said, 'Proper George Cox.'

When we got out of the shop, with me holding Dad's creepers in their box in a bag, I said to Dad, 'What accent did that girl have?'

'Geordie,' said Dad.

The world had not stopped turning while I'd been away. All these faces coming towards me as I walked along the High Street towards the Lock. People I recognized who recognized me. They didn't know something had happened since they last saw me, that they weren't seeing the same person.

A wing had fallen off the silver aeroplane that was about to crash into the pavement. It had crashed before it had crashed.

Then I saw Sue Blass. I couldn't believe it. And not just Sue. She was with Barry Lunc's brother—and Monster himself. They were walking up from Inverness Street, coming into the High Street at right angles to me. Barry's brother had his arm round Sue Blass and Barry was following a few paces behind. She'd had her belly button pierced and was wearing a Che Guevara top. Dad had a Che Guevara lapel badge. Mum had chucked that too. I just stood there as they came up to me. I managed to put a grin on my face, a grin I hoped would say I was happy and cool. But I needn't have bothered because their eyes looked right through me, they blew through me as if they were wind and I was smoke.

You won't believe what I did next. I went and stood in front of a shop window to check I was visible and that I still looked like me and not like some manure muncher on day release from Manuresville who's come to Camden to buy a bag of marijuana which is really dried herbs for about thirty quid.

It had stopped raining but was getting a bit cold and as I walked up Inverness Street I got my fleece out of my backpack and put it on. I passed Out On The Floor Records, which is probably where Barry, Barry's brother, and Sue Blass had been, and some hustlers selling dodgy grass, and turned left into Gloucester Crescent.

There was scaffolding on the front of our house, and a skip in the front garden. I felt angry. What was so bad about our house, that someone had to have loads of work done on it? I stood in the street looking up at the windows of our house, looking for signs of life. A girl wearing a parka walked past. I didn't pay her any attention. Then she turned into our drive and walked up the steps to the front door of our house. She rang the bell of our house. While she was waiting she turned round and stared at me. After a few seconds the front door of our house opened. I saw a woman in a dressing gown with a towel piled on her head. The woman hugged the girl, then the girl said something and the woman looked over her shoulder at me. Our front door closed.

I carried on standing there. The woman's face appeared at a downstairs window. She had taken the towel off her head. Her face disappeared. Maybe she was calling the cops. But there was no law to say you couldn't stand in a road looking at your own house.

On the other hand, maybe the cops would realize I matched the description they must have of the kid who battered the Gobber and they might arrest me for that.

I walked down by the canal, sat on a bench and had another muesli bar and a packet of cheese and onion crisps. I made sure it wasn't the same bench I'd been sitting on when I monged the Gobber. Then I remembered that there wasn't even a possibility that the Gobber was dead because Barry had seen him since, and that cheered me up a bit because it meant that I may be turning into a manure muncher with the Bozo's genes running around my body wearing little cravats, and the person I loved as my dad may have finally conked out on me and I may have a bastard brother and my mum may be the world's biggest betrayer, but at least I wasn't a murderer, or even a manslaughterer.

People were going home. I could tell by the way they walked, with a purpose in their step. They were probably going to watch telly and have a slice of pizza. Maybe they were going to try on a piece of kit like a jacket they'd bought at the Lock at the weekend and

186

were waiting for the right time to wear. The only people not going home were the dossers and me.

Dossers look away if you stare them in the eyes. A five-year-old kid can outstare a dosser.

Where the canal turns a sharp corner, I walked up the steps to the road, crossed the canal on the foot-bridge, crossed the Outer Circle of Regent's Park, and walked down towards the wolf enclosure. I felt excited. I remembered again what Dad had said about the sea and hills, how they draw you towards them. The fire in wolves' skulls was drawing me in.

# Chapter 14

When Dad was in bed in his downstairs study—when he was dying, in other words, but we never mentioned the D-word (or the SD-word, which stands for life is Shit and then you Die)—I used to go and see the wolves every day. Come out of school, get the bus down to Camden High Street and walk along the canal to the park. Hang out with the wolves for a bit then walk home, my heart beating faster as I got near the house and wondered what had happened that day. Because something had always happened. His catheter bag had leaked or the district nurse had called out the doc because his blood pressure was low, or, once, he saw a face on the ceiling and it wouldn't go away.

The things that happened were never good, of course, because every day he was getting worse, he was dying a bit more. Except for once. Once, something amazing happened.

It was really cold that day, so cold the edges of the canal had frozen. The ducks couldn't work it out. As I walked along the towpath I watched them trying to walk on the ice and falling over. The wolves were cool about the cold though because they came from the frozen north.

188

There were eight of them visible, more than I'd ever seen out of their tunnel at one time. Eight breaths pluming in the wild cold air. Some of them stood, noses up, others turned and trotted and stopped. And trotted. All sniffed the air, smelling the Arctic coming towards them. A couple of them gave me that sweet-wrapper look.

Something was different, something was changing. That's what they told me. I watched my breath plume, and I felt it too.

Walking back along Gloucester Crescent, a sense almost of excitement. The street lights were shining on bike saddles. A bonfire smell, brake lights where the road rises towards the T-junction, a cat flattened on a wall, watching me pass.

Dad was fine, you wouldn't have known there was anything wrong (except for him being in bed downstairs, and looking like an anorexic, and being attached to a wee bag).

He laid down the book he was reading. It was the book of poems he'd been reading before. It had a bright orange and yellow cover that looked like a close-up photograph of a fire. 'So what's happening, kidder?' he said. Dad's face looked at the ceiling as he spoke, but his eyes looked at me.

'Elvis is alive. Not a lot.'

'Glad to hear it. Where you bin?'

'In the park for a bit.'

'Regent's Park?'

I nodded. I hadn't told him before about going to see the wolves. I was embarrassed because he'd suspect that me wanting to see the wolves all the time was about him being ill and how much it upset me. But now I told him, because it seemed right, I still felt how beautiful they had looked in the cold, darkening light. 'Checking out the wolves,' I said.

'You're kidding me.'

'No I'm not.'

He seemed excited. He tried to sit up. 'Hey, Clare,' he shouted. 'Clare.'

Mum came to the door. She was holding a leek as if it was a sword.

Dad said, 'Guess where Davy Crockett here has been?'

Mum said, 'Amaze me.'

Dad said, 'Only to see the wolves in Regent's Park, that's all.'

Mum raised her eyebrows, not getting it. I didn't get it either.

'And what have I been reading this afternoon, at exactly the same time kidder was outside the wolf enclosure? Only a poem about the wolves in Regent's Park zoo, that's all. Here, listen.' And Dad picked up the book with the flaming fire cover and read out some lines about the moons of February and March and being consoled by the howling of wolves.

The red plastic tape should have told me what had happened. I saw it from up near the entrance to the park. I was walking quickly, imagining the wolf communication I was about to do. Sometimes, when I got

190

to the enclosure, there was no sign of a wolf. They were underground, in their tunnel. It might take forty minutes for one to come out, but I didn't mind. I'd just stand there, by the fence, waiting. It was a good kind of waiting, like the waiting for a Thai curry in that little Thai place in Kentish Town when Dad allows you two sips of his cold beer.

As I got nearer I saw there was a large yellow earth-mover with caterpillar tracks in the wolf enclosure. I ran the last few metres to the fence. Now I understood the red plastic tape. It was the sort of tape they put around building sites. The wolf enclosure was a building site. They were destroying it. In fact it wasn't a wolf enclosure any more. The driver of the earth-mover had already gone home, leaving the earth-mover tilted halfway up the mound that had contained the wolf tunnel. Half the mound had already gone. The timbers that had made the tunnel were lying on the ground, splintered and smashed.

I ran round to the zoo entrance. It started to drizzle and about three hundred Japanese tourists were putting their anoraks on at the same time. I found a bloke in a white shirt and said, 'Do you work at the zoo?' and he said yes.

'What's happened to the wolves?'

'They've gone.'

'I know. When are they coming back?'

'They're not coming back. They've been moved to Whipsnade Wildlife Park.'

'Never coming back?'

'No. The ostriches are going where the wolves used to be.'

'Ostriches?'

'That's right. Excuse me.' A Japanese woman had come up to him with a map.

I set off back towards what used to be the wolf enclosure. It was raining harder now. I turned into the park and tried to walk under trees so they sheltered me. Then the rain got so heavy that I stopped walking and stood close up to this tree trunk, trying to get as much protection as possible. It didn't feel so good to be out in the rain now. It didn't feel like NOTHING MATTERED. When the rain had eased off a bit I ran back to the zoo entrance and tried to find the bloke in the white shirt but he wasn't there. I found a woman in a white shirt instead and said to her, 'Excuse me, where is Whipsnade Wildlife Park?'

'Whipsnade? It's in Bedfordshire.'

'Where's that? How do you get there? What time does it close?'

'Whooaa, steady on. You get your mum or dad to drive you, is the best bet.'

'I haven't got a dad.'

'Oh, I'm sorry. Well. Ask your mum to take you.'

I don't know why, but I said, 'She's in the toilet.' Then I said, 'What time does Whipsnade close?'

'I think it's six in the summer.' I looked at my watch. It was five fifteen. The woman laughed. 'You won't get there today,' she said.

* * *

I sat on a bench in the park. I ate another muesli bar, some cheese from its opened packet, and a bag of crisps and I drank the carton of Ribena. I got my mobile out and wondered whether to switch it on. Would Mum know yet that I'd gone missing? Probably not. Even if she'd rung the cottage and I didn't answer, she'd think I was out on my bike. It was five forty now. She'd be getting home in the next half hour. Give it another hour after that, say seven fifteen, and she'd start to panic.

And the first thing she'd do? Call the Bozo.

It had stopped raining but it was still cold. The park was almost empty.


It was eight forty-five, getting dark. A bloke in a green uniform came walking along. He stopped. 'Are you OK, son? Are you on your own?'

'I'm with my mum but she's gone to find a toilet.'

The bloke looked a bit puzzled. He stared around, and hesitated, and said, 'OK, well, the gates are closing in ten minutes so she hasn't got long. Where did she go?'

'That way.' I pointed towards the Camden side of the park. 'I'll go and find her.'

'Take care then,' said the bloke. But he didn't move on, he stood there watching me while I loaded my backpack and set off. After going about fifty metres I turned round and he was still watching me. He waved and I waved back. Next time I looked, he'd gone.

I veered off the path and headed for some bushes. I crawled in among them. In the middle was a body-shaped dip covered in dead leaves. I lay down to try it out. It was very comfortable. I was suddenly incredibly tired. I could have closed my eyes and just fallen asleep but I made myself sit up. I got Grandpa's Swiss Army knife out of the backpack and fiddled around with it, waiting for the point of no return. The point of no return was when they locked the gates. I pulled out the corkscrew on the penknife and screwed it into the ground. I looked up through the leaves and branches.

Even though it was almost dark, the sky looked quite bright compared to the branches. Then I saw the moon. I got Grandpa's binoculars out and looked at the moon through them. It was amazing. It was silver and a bit battered, like the buckle on the belt that Dad got from Keith Richards and that Mum chucked.

Nine fifteen. By now, I knew, the park gates had been locked and Mum would be in a major panic. I laid down my head on the pillow of leaves and closed my eyes.

Mum was quite clever about it all, as she told me a long time afterwards when the world had straightened up again. She forced herself to think. Where might Mungo have gone? Vern's house (no). Barry's house (way). Gloucester Crescent. Camden Lock. The canal. My God, the canal. Hampstead Heath.

Of course the Bozo got involved. He came round to the cottage and called PC Strickland. The man who spewed cauliflower cheese instead of words talked to Camden Town Plod and they sent coppers out to the Heath, in particular Parly Hill, and no I wasn't there. Think, think. Anywhere else?

'Maybe Regent's Park,' Mum said. 'He used to love going there to see the wolves.'

Camden Town Plod talked to Parks Plod and the boy who had probably been sliced by a paedo and left for dead on the Regent's Canal towpath had come back to life.


The parks policewoman put me in the back seat, pulled a blanket from the boot and put that round me. She said to the parks policeman, 'Get the engine started and turn the heater up.'

The parks policeman turned the ignition on and the heater came on full-blast except it was cold air, not warm, at first. He picked the walkie-talkie off the dash and was saying, 'Yeah, we got him. In Regent's Park. In a bush. That's right. Cold and wet and sorry for himself but otherwise . . . Of course.' He handed the walkie-talkie over his shoulder to me. 'Here, son. Talk to your mother.'

I put the walkie-talkie to my ear. Mum said, 'Oh, love. Oh, thank God. I'll be there as quick as I can. Are you all right? What happened? It doesn't matter what happened. All that matters is that you're all right. You are all right?'

And then I remembered. 'They took the wolves away,' I said.

* * *

The policewoman gave me a lecture about how lucky I'd been not to be picked up by a paedo or a nutter. Then she asked me if I was having trouble at home, and did I want to talk about it, but no way was I going to discuss my mother's sex life and my illegitimate brother with a parks policewoman, so I just said, 'My dad's died.'

On the way back to Manuresville with Mum, I tried not to speak. I could feel her getting angry, then trying to stop herself. She knew she shouldn't be angry with me. I'd just spent a night sleeping rough in London and I was only fifteen. I could have been sliced up by a nutter. 'Please, Mungo,' she said, 'please tell me what's going on. I won't be angry, I promise. But I need to know what the problem is so we can start trying to put it right.'

'I told you. They took the wolves away.'

'What does that mean? Tell me what that means, Mungo. Help me so I can help you. So we can help each other.'

'They've got rid of the wolf enclosure at the zoo. That's what it means. I asked them at the zoo and they said the wolves have gone to Whipsnade. So that's it.' I looked out of the window at the fag end of London. Billboards and flyovers and the first fields. Manure Land in the offing.

196

'Oh, love.' Mum put her left hand on my right shoulder.

I lifted my shoulder and shrugged off her hand. That was another way Mum and I could talk, by just-touching and not-touching.

'You slept in a ditch full of water. That's a very lonely thing for a young man to do. Why did you do that? You must tell me.'

'It was dry when I went to sleep,' I said. 'I didn't deliberately lie in a wet ditch. I'm not stupid.'

Mum didn't reply to this. I stared ahead at the grey surface and blue signs of the motorway, and the fields and trees on either side. We were in full-blown Manuresville now. Not many cars taking the happy road to Manure Land with us at seven o'clock in the morning. I imagined the motorway being vertical, not horizontal. We were speeding at 77mph in a Skoda deeper and deeper underground. How mad was this, that we couldn't wait to bury ourselves alive?

Every so often, when Mum overtook another car, the indicator ticked like an insect in a hedge.

Mum took a deep breath, as if she was going to speak, then let the breath out without saying anything. Another deep breath—and this time she dived in. 'Mungo, believe me, I haven't underestimated what it must be like for a young man to lose his—'

'Bullshit.'

Mum kept dead calm. She was leaning forward on her seat and staring through the windscreen as if she was concentrating on the broken white lines painted on the

197

carriageway. 'You will hear me out on this. You don't have to say anything but you will listen to what your mother—because that's who I am, your mother, with all the responsibilities that that entails—you will show me the respect of listening to what I have to say. OK?'

'No,' I said. 'Not OK. I don't give a monkey's what you have to say cos I've heard it all before and it's bullshit and I know about my bastard brother and who my real father is OK so you don't have to lie any more.'

I looked out of the side window at big letters painted on the side of a truck dumped in a field: PICK YOUR OWN STRAWB'S NEXT EXIT.

Silence. The indicator ticking again. Then Mum said, 'Pardon?'

'You heard,' I said. 'No wonder you moved to Manuresville after Dad died. You wanted to be near them both.'

'What on earth are you talking about?'

But I kept silent. I wasn't playing her games just as I wouldn't play Mungo's.

'Our exit's just here,' Mum said. 'Give me a minute and we'll get to the bottom of this.'

The indicator ticked, the Skoda slowed and took off on a leftward trajectory from the motorway. Traffic lights which changed to green as we reached them. A layby. We slowed and stopped. Ahead of us a bloke was unloading flowers from the back of a van and arranging them on a stall.

Mum turned off the ignition and twisted towards me, trying to stroke my hair. I pulled my head away, thumping the back of it against the passenger window. She sighed and put her hands in her lap. 'Now what are you trying to say to me?' she said. 'Did I hear you say you think you have a brother?'

'I *know* I have,' I said. 'I've met him. So don't give me any bullshit.'

'All right, all right,' Mum said. 'So what's his name, this brother of yours?'

'You know what his name is.'

'Remind me.'

'This is ridiculous,' I said. 'You can't get out of it.'

'Just tell me his name.'

'MUNGO!' I shouted. 'Satisfied?'

Mum put her head in her hands. 'Oh, love,' she said. '*You're* Mungo.' She reached for me again and this time I didn't have the energy to stop her. And as she stroked my hair I told her the other part of the secret, that the Bozo was my real father.

She squeezed me so tight I thought I'd suffocate. 'Oh, love,' she said, 'what a terrible thing to think. How could you believe that, even for a second? You're *so* like your father it's not true. What about your green eyes, like him? Your curly hair, like him? Your lovely nose, your . . . your *gobbiness*, for God's sake? There's only one person that could have come from. Eh?'

My eyes were making her top wet. After a while Mum lifted my head away from her slightly and said, 'This is good. This is very good. You know, you've never really cried for your dad before. You had a bit of a blub the day he died but ever since then you've held it in, haven't you? Even the day of the funeral. You were great, I was very proud of you. But a person can be *too* great sometimes. Even you.'

Two days later we were back in London, at the bereavement counsellor's in Belsize Park where I'd gone after Dad died. I had three sessions after he died. The counsellor had an amazing blue chin from having to shave so much, smooth and blue like a plum with a cleft in it. He wasn't a bad bloke but he didn't know much about kids, which was a drawback seeing as he specialized in talking to them. I mean you could easily bullshit him. He talked about anger and how important it was to get it out, and at the end of the third session he invited my mum into the room and said I was showing remarkable maturity for a fifteen year old whose Dad had recently popped his creepers.

A week after that I battered the Gobber almost to death. But hey, I got my anger out so what's the problem?

This time around, we went to talk about my troubled summer. 'Mungo has been having a troubled summer,' Mum told him. And she went through the various stuff about moving to a completely new environment and not knowing anyone and the difficult day I had when my London friends came to visit and the running away, and then (no mention of the Bozo, I noticed) she got down to the thing that was really bothering her—bothering both of us. 'I think,' Mum said almost under her breath, 'there has been a bit of a confusion between reality and fantasy in Mungo's mind. He always did have a fertile imagination. His father used to say—'

'Please,' I said.

'Anyway,' Mum went on, 'he's been spending so much time on his own, to the point where—well, tell Dr Cousins, Mungo, what you told me.'

'I met this boy who I thought was my brother,' I said. 'And he told me—well he didn't exactly tell me, but he sort of showed me—that my dad wasn't really my dad, he was his dad, who is called Brian Boland.'

Mum looked at the doc and said, 'It's confusing, I know.'

'And this isn't true?' said the doc to Mum.

Mum shook her head as hard as she could without getting a nosebleed. 'Tell Dr Cousins what you think this boy is called,' she said.

I shrugged. 'Mungo. That's what he said anyway.'

The doc stuck his finger in the hole in his chin and said to me, 'Has there been anyone else present when you've seen this boy, Mungo?'

It was a good question. 'No,' I had to admit.

'But you're convinced he exists? He's as real as I am, sitting here?'

I shrugged again. I honestly didn't know any more.

Then the doc went on about how it was relatively common for kids at some stage to question if one or other of their parents was their real, biological parent. In my case the trauma of bereavement had perhaps brought this on. He said he didn't want to get into medical terms but what I'd gone through was certainly big enough to have led to an emotional splitting off which in turn could lead to—he coughed at this point and put his hand over his mouth, trying to speak to Mum without me understanding (duh!)—which could lead to (*cough*) 'psychotic delusions'.

A slimehead, a mong, and now a psycho!

The GP came to the cottage and gave me some pills and I stayed in bed for two days, watching daytime TV on a portable that the Bozo had probably brought round and was probably Tally's reject but I didn't ask.

I said to Mum, 'So you promise my dad's my dad and I don't have a brother, that Mungo doesn't exist?'

'Promise,' she said. 'There's only one Mungo and he's sitting right in front of me looking like he needs a bath and a change of pyjamas.'

I shook my head, thinking of the moment I'd lost it and battered the Gobber. Then I started to cry. 'But that means I'm mad,' I said. 'I'm a psycho with psychotic delusions who invents people and things and . . . and—' I was going to add: 'nearly kills kids with special needs' but I stopped myself.

'Shush, shush,' said Mum and put her cool hand on my hot forehead. 'It's nobody's business except ours. And it's completely understandable, that's what Doctor Cousins said, given all you've been through and what an unusual young man you are. Your father always said you had a mind like a multiplex.'

I'm not sure, by the way, I ever really believed that what Mum and Doc Cousins said was true, that I'd made it all up. But sometimes it's easier to go along with what everyone else thinks and ignore what *you* know and think, especially if you're afraid of what you know and think.

I didn't forget the jellyfish, of course I didn't. I knew I couldn't have invented that too. And any time I wanted I could verify its existence: all I had to do was go through to Mum's bedroom when she popped out. The jellyfish was real, but the moment had gone. I didn't want to ask questions any more.

Besides, it was the wolves that made me fight and now they'd disappeared, and I was starting to think that maybe it was wrong to fight, to fight against the bullshit that life dumped on me. Best to stand there and take the manure that was shovelled on my head because what was so special about me? Anyone would think I was the only one having to take it. But that was what life was, that was what history was—a million billion people each with their very own farm-yard hopper dangling above them dropping industrial

203

quantities of manure on them night and day. You can't fight manure, you can't punch it and if you yell at it, it'll only land in your mouth (and then you'll be a manure muncher—ha ha). Realizing this was called growing up.

I pulled the duvet up around my head and laughed at a television advert for stairlifts.

# Chapter 15

Ten days to go to the start of term in my new school. Mum and I were being what Dad called shiny happy people. We didn't talk about Dad dying, or Mungo, or me running away, we only talked about the future. Mum took me into Basingstoke to get my new uniform (don't ask). She said it was going to be a new start all round, that when I'd been at school for a week everything that had happened this year would seem like a bad dream.

A week to go to the start of term—and Bickleigh was in the path of Britain's first official hurricane.

For days a deep depression had been heading in from the Atlantic. TV news showed satellite pictures of it swirling towards us and gave warnings about which areas were likely to be most affected. It came in across the coast during the night and whizzed up through central southern England, hitting Bickleigh at about three a.m.

All the previous evening the wind had been getting up and there were TV news flashes that interrupted normal programmes to give updates. Mum and I stayed downstairs in our dressing gowns, watching TV and feeling in a peculiar mood, half-scared and half-excited. At midnight the TV switched to a permanent news programme and that was when they first mentioned that the storm had been officially upgraded to a hurricane.

Winds were gusting at up to one hundred and thirty mph. The tops of the stands at St Mary's football stadium in Southampton were ripped off. Windows and bits of panelling blew off the Spinnaker Tower in Portsmouth and killed three people on the ground. People were warned to stay indoors and do what they could to secure their homes. Mum hugged me and I headbutted her shoulder like the zombified sheep I'd become.

'We'll be all right,' she said, adding, 'I think,' as if she didn't believe herself. 'We're in a bit of a dip here. It should go across the top of us. Shall we have a peek outside?'

We went to the garden door together and Mum had to struggle to open it. Outside, the air was swerving and charging round the garden, bending bushes and tossing plant pots around. It knocked us back, it knocked the breath out of us, it made us laugh and it made us frightened. In the darkness, the wind was booming in the trees around the house. It sounded like a recording of crashing waves, slowed right down. I helped Mum pull the door closed.

'Phew,' she said. 'I've never known anything like that. This climate change business is for real. I think we stay down here together tonight, just in case. What do you think?'

'In case of what?'

'Well, I'm sure it won't happen but—'

'But what?'

'Well, you never know. It's possible a tree could come down on top of us. So best to be on the safe side, eh?'

We kept the TV on with the sound turned low and made a nest on the sofa with rugs and cushions and a tray with tea and biscuits on it. Then, at about one a.m., the electricity went off, the lights and TV died. 'Oh no,' said Mum. We stared at the blank TV screen, watching the glow fade. After about a minute the lights and TV flickered, on-off, on-off, then came on again properly. 'Thank God,' said Mum.

A minute later the electricity went off again, and this time it stayed off. The booming of the wind in the trees sounded extra-loud in the dark.

After five minutes of us sitting there not saying anything, just listening to the wind and imagining this whirlpool of angry air moving towards us across the hills and fields, Mum said, half to herself and half to me, 'Think, think. Where would Grandma have kept the candles?'

'In the cupboard under the sink?'

'Good lad. I bet that's where they are. Now it's just a question of getting there in the pitch black.'

'Hey,' I said, 'remember that cave we went in in Barbados? *That* was dark. I can still see the outlines of things a bit here.' We were about to be hit by the worst storm ever to hit Britain, and I was all curled up on a sofa with tea and biccies feeling chilled as hell.

'I'm glad you can. I can't see a thing. Do you mind looking for the candles then? And hopefully there should be matches there too, otherwise I don't know what we'll do.'

'OK.'

I felt my way towards the kitchen, trying to remember the lay-out of the room. When I reached the door I couldn't find the handle. I felt the door in every place that the handle could possibly be but it wasn't there. I started to laugh.

'What's so funny?'

'Since the electricity went off somebody must have broken into the house and very silently nicked the door handle cos it ain't here. Oh, hang about. Here it is.'

I found the candles, and some matches, and brought three saucers to stand the candles in. We sat there in the candlelight and listened to the wind, and I started to doze off with my head on Mum's shoulder. Mum stroked my hair a few times, which I didn't encourage but I didn't stop her either, and soon we were both dozing.

A pattering noise woke us both up. 'What's that?' said Mum.

I knew what it was. 'Rain. I get it in the grate in my room too, when it's heavy enough.'

We listened. Beyond the pattering in the fireplace, over and above the booming of the wind in the trees, there was the loud hissing of heavy rain. Over the next hour the booming and hissing grew louder, the windows and doors rattled, and even the walls of the cottage seemed to shake. Every so often there'd be a sliding-crunching sound from above, then a smashing noise on the flagstones outside. The roof tiles were coming down. We weren't dozing now. We weren't exactly hugging each other, our arms were too rigid for that, but we were bracing each other, as if the wind was actually booming through that room and we were doing all we could to stop ourselves being blown away.

Mum's eyes looked huge in the candlelight. She had an idea. 'Get the radio,' she said. 'Maybe the radio's still transmitting. Maybe the army'll come and rescue us.'

I brought the radio in from the kitchen and switched it on but there was just white noise. Mum twiddled the tuner, then gave up. 'No chance. I wonder if the phone's still working.'

I went back into the kitchen and tried the phone. 'Dead as a dead man's dick,' I said.

'Mungo!' said Mum.

I returned to the sofa and we didn't say anything for a while, just held on to each other and listened to the storm—the hurricane—getting louder and angrier. Then Mum said in a whisper, 'It's amazing really.'

'What?' I was whispering too.

'Being cut off like this. No electricity, no phone, no radio, no TV. No information. It's too dangerous to go out. It makes you feel like—I don't know. A dot of nothing.'

Neither of us spoke for a while, then I said, 'Mum—' and stopped.

'Yes?'

'Do you ever wonder why you're you?'

'How d'you mean?'

'I mean, as opposed to somebody else. Say, Mrs Plunkett-Strawberry. If all you are is a speck of nothing, you may as well be Mrs Plunkett-Strawberry. So why are you you and not her?'

'Well—'

I could tell she didn't get it. 'Or,' I said, 'why am I me and not a million other kids? Say, if you hadn't married Dad but someone else, and you had a kid, would that kid still be me? Or would it be half-me?'

'Oh no, Mungo, don't start on about that again. We've got enough on our plate at the moment. You know, I think that rain is getting even heavier. And there goes another roof tile. What are we going to do? Maybe we should go down to the cellar.'

'If you had had a kid, but with a different husband, what would you have called it?'

'I've told you that before. My first boy was always going to be called Mungo. Do you think we should go down to the cellar?'

'So if you hadn't been in that recording studio in Marylebone on the same day as Dad, I wouldn't exist. And then you'd have met another bloke, maybe a racing driver or a foreign correspondent, and had a kid and that kid would be Mungo, but he wouldn't be me, would he? Or would he?'

Mum stroked my hair. 'Please, love. We're not in a very good situation here and I don't know what to do.'

Suddenly I knew, with the storm raging outside, the moment had come to ask the question. 'Mum, why have you got a—?'

I was going to say 'Dutch cap under the bed'—but at that moment the tree came down on the house.

The tree karate-chopped the roof and the house shook so much we thought it was about to collapse, like the house of straw blown down by a wolf. Mum screamed and hugged me. I screwed my eyes tight shut, waiting to be covered and crushed. The cottage seemed to tilt. I heard pictures sliding down the walls. We could have been in the ballroom of the *Titanic*, half an hour before sinking. We both started coughing. When I opened my eyes it was pitch black, the candles had been knocked over and extinguished. I tasted dust on my tongue and inadvertently hoovered dust into my throat so I coughed and coughed, unable to catch my breath.

Mum hugged me even tighter. 'Oh my God, oh my God, this is it. Shall we try and get down to the cellar, what d'you think?'

The entrance to the cellar was a trapdoor behind the

sofa we were huddled on. I said, 'But then if something fell on the trapdoor, we'd be trapped.'

'That's true. Where've the candles gone, can you find them?'

I felt around on the table till I found one of the candles, which I put back on its saucer and lit. We looked around the room. There were gaps where pictures had hung. Dust escaped like smoke from the cracks between ceiling and walls. We flapped our hands in front of our faces, trying to fan away the dust, and Mum said between coughs, 'What about just getting under the table there? It's solid enough.'

So we crawled under the living room table and stayed there, wrapped in rugs, listening to the cottage creaking and groaning, listening to the wind booming and the rain hissing, listening out for the sudden crack-and-splinter of another tree coming down.

Eventually the wind and rain seemed to lessen a bit. The house didn't groan quite so much, the dust had died down. I ventured out from under the table to open the curtains. Behind them, the oblongs of window were pale with the beginning of day. I crawled back under the table and Mum said in a whisper, 'I don't want to tempt fate, but I think the worst is over. You were wonderful, love. Cup of tea? I'll put a pan on to boil.'

* * *

We didn't know it then, but we got off lightly. In Bickleigh itself, forty-seven houses were completely destroyed and one person was killed. It was the worst concentration of damage anywhere except for on the coast. For the first time ever, the Town of Dead People came alive, except for the poor manure muncher walking his dog who was flattened by a lamppost.

But that morning we had no way of contacting anybody or finding anything out. We had some cereal and got dressed, and by then the wind had dropped and the rain had slowed to a drizzle and we reckoned it was safe to go outside though Mum found some old riding hats and made us wear those, in case of falling debris. We opened the door.

The fallen tree swooped over us like a flyover. We walked underneath it and stood in the middle of the garden looking back at the house. The tree had smashed a V in the roof. I looked at Mum, and Mum shuddered and hugged me, thinking the same thing: if we'd been in our beds, one if not both of us would have been killed. The roof timbers were splintered like snapped matchsticks and a shower of tiles lay on the ground all round the cottage.

Mum said, 'Here's what we're going to do. You're going to stay here in case anybody like the police or the army turn up, and keep your riding hat on—no buts, Mungo. You keep the hat on. No one can see you, for God's sake! And I'm going to take the Skoda and see how far I get and what I can find out. OK, love?'

213

'OK,' I said. One thing I was pleased about: she hadn't decided to just sit there and wait for the Bozo to turn up like the Eighth Armoured Division.

Of course I took the riding hat off straight away. I waited fifteen minutes. Inside me the wolves were back, energized by the hurricane. I went up the stairs, taking it carefully in case the roof came down on my head, and went into Mum's bedroom. I looked for the jellyfish. Under the bed, in the cupboard, in the drawers. No jellyfish. Mum must have it on her. Why did she have it on her? Maybe because she suspected I'd been snooping around. Or maybe for quick usage, any place any time.

The lane outside the cottage was in a bad state. The rain had turned one side of it into a rushing river. I had to slow the mountain bike almost to a standstill to weave around the fallen branches and stones and the occasional tree trunk slewed right across the middle. I couldn't see how Mum could have driven this way in a crappy Skoda. Then I turned the corner and had my answer. The Skoda was parked at the side of the road; or not exactly parked, just stopped, half on the road and half on the muddy bank. I cycled up as fast as I could, yelling, 'Mum, Mum!'

The Skoda was empty.

I tried the doors. They were locked. I couldn't work it out. Then I could. This was Bozo business, had to be. Mum had probably taken about fifteen minutes to go two hundred metres down this road. Then she'd met the Bozo coming the other way in his 4WD, doing his Eighth Armoured Division impersonation, and she had got in with him and driven off deep into the wreckage of Manuresville.

I hesitated, wondering whether to go back or continue towards Bickleigh. Then I heard a car coming slowly up the hill and I had time to crouch down with the bike behind Mum's car. As I'd thought, it was the bozomobile, and Mum was in the passenger seat. The Bozo was revving the engine and enjoying riding over the obstacles. I stayed next to the Skoda, waiting for the bozomobile to return. Ten minutes later I heard it coming and crouched back down out of sight. Mum was still in the passenger seat. Work that one out.

I cycled back to the cottage. There was a notice pinned on the front door in Mum's handwriting. It said:

Mungo, where on earth are you? Do not enter the cottage. I've been told it is almost certainly now a dangerous structure. Please come to Bickleigh village hall on your bike and meet me there. You don't need to bring anything (except the riding hat!). There is clothing and bedding and food in Bickleigh. So, repeat, do not on any account enter the cottage. Come as soon as you can, love. And take care.

Mum xxxx

# Chapter 16

In the distance the white gateposts of the Pineapple House came into view. I didn't think anything of it at first. I was too busy riding round and over the obstacles lying in the road—a mobile barbecue, a deflated paddling pool, wellington boots, and sludgy trails of mud in snakeskin patterns—and hiding from the occasional car. Once, the Bozo drove past again—minus Mum, this time—but three times it was the police, going really slowly with headlights on and blue light flashing but no siren. I really didn't fancy being picked up by PC Toe-Cheese-Spouter or his mates, even in the unusual circumstances of Manuresville having just been flattened by Britain's first dictionary-definition hurricane.

As I got nearer the pineapple gateposts I could hear a smashing sound as tiles slid from the roof of the bungalow—or what I assumed was the bungalow. But when I looked through the gates towards the house the bungalow had disappeared. No rusting car wrecks, no neon santa. In their place, a big white house with battlements along the top that seemed immediately familiar, even though I was sure I had never seen it before. I stopped and stared, trying to work it out. Maybe there were *two* houses with pineapples on the gate-posts and I just hadn't noticed this one until now. I looked up and down the Bickleigh Road. There was definitely only one set of pineapple gateposts.

In my heart, wolves were stirring and sniffing. It was true that I had not seen this house before, but I still knew it. I had been in it. That was it. In the nightmare I had had down the well.

I stared at the white house with battlements, my heart thumping hard in my chest. I told myself this must be a psychotic delusion. But nothing had ever seemed more real. This wasn't a made-up thing screening in the cinema of my head. Here was the drive that the Bozo had driven into in his Land Rover, the front door he had walked through in his wellies. That big window on the first floor—that must be my bedroom window where I had stood and watched the Bozo arriving.

The roof had been badly damaged and tiles were still falling off and plinking to the ground. In the drive was a Jag with a personalized number plate: BOL A1. BOL equalled Boland. Brian Boland. This was the Bozo's house. But how could it be? The Bozo lived at Hedge End Hall. I walked up to the front door. A notice was drawing-pinned there:

POLICE NOTICE
**UNSAFE STRUCTURE**
_DO NOT ENTER_

I rang the bell just in case. No reply. I knocked the heavy lion's head knocker. Not a sound except for the wind roaring in the treetops all around and, from inside, faint smashing and creaking sounds, as if the house was slowly collapsing.

Bickleigh is a small town of very old houses, so old their roofs have sunken into wavy lines. They were sitting ducks for the hurricane. It had got them, one by one. Cracked in the roofs, blown out the windows, picked up cars and slotted them through letterboxes, like a mafia hitman leaving a calling card. Bits of building were still falling off or sliding down. I cycled carefully in the middle of the road, making slow progress among all the debris.

The low sound of a crowd of people talking. The road turned at a right angle into the high street. The village hall was on the left, a large square building with a noticeboard next to the entrance advertising Mrs Plunkett-Strawberry's horseshit about the wells of old Wessex. The hurricane had shredded the Union Jack on the flagpole above the entrance and blown out most of the windows. I could see heads moving behind the cracked glass. They looked unattached, like a jam of objects bobbing in a tank. There were more people, maybe a hundred or so, in front of the open double doors of the hall, on the steps leading up to the doors and in the road, and it was their muttered conversations I had heard before I turned the corner.

I set off through the crowd, peering at the faces, looking for Mum and trying to remember not to be rude to the Bozo if he was with her. And when I had found Mum I was going to take her back to the Pineapple House, immediately, before it had a chance to change. I was going to show it to her to prove I wasn't mad, the world was mad instead. But that wasn't my problem.

People looked in a state of shock, as expressionless as statues. An elderly couple stood side by side, not talking. The bloke was holding an umbrella above both of them. As I walked towards him he completely ignored me, staring straight ahead and fiddling with his tie with his spare hand. The woman was also staring ahead.

'Excuse me,' I said. 'Have you seen Mrs McFall? She works in the charity shop.'

'I wish we could go home,' said the woman.

I thought she was talking to me and I started to reply: 'Oh right, well I'm sure—'

But the bloke talked right over me, saying, 'There are two perfectly good camp beds waiting for us in there.'

And I realized they hadn't noticed me. But even then I didn't understand what was going on. I just thought it was because they were the usual half-dead Bickleigh manure munchers. And you couldn't blame them for being extra-zombified when the most amazing thing since dinosaurs lived here had just happened.

Other people were losing their tempers. A woman holding a newspaper over her head against the rain stamped her foot as I passed and shouted out, 'This is intolerable, absolutely intolerable. Why doesn't somebody do something?'

A man replied, 'Such as remain calm and patient and supportive of our emergency services, who are doing their usual magnificent job, I'm sure, and the last thing they need is people carping.' Somebody laughed. Somebody else gave the man a round of applause. Then things fell quiet and tense again.

'Excuse me—' I said, but nobody even looked in my direction.

A familiar whiff came wafting through the crowd: the Smelly Man. I didn't see him at first because he was sitting down. He was wearing his cardigan and had a snout on the go, with his hand umbrellaed over the top of it, and he was looking up at the bloke standing next to him, who was dressed in a cop uniform and holding a megaphone. It was the Toe-Cheese-Spouter, aka PC Strickland. Mrs Toe-Cheese—Miss Strickland—was just behind them. I half-thought of going up to her and saying in a London voice, 'Seen your bungalow lately then? Cos it don't exist no more. Just thought you'd like to know.'

Then the Smelly Man stared straight at me and I froze, looking around for an escape route. But I needn't have bothered. He just shook his head and switched his gaze back to PC Strickland, who raised the megaphone to his mouth.

'Ladies and gentlemen,' said the Toe-Cheese-Spouter into the megaphone, which made an electronic shriek.

'Ladies and—' He coughed. 'Thank you for your patience and your . . . your—I think we can safely call it the Dunkirk spirit, ha! ha! Just to reiterate. The village hall has been passed safe so do feel free to wait in it or remain near it. Other structures are almost certainly dangerous so please watch yourselves, I will convey information as and when I have it. In the meantime I would ask you all to remain where you are and . . . er . . . await information. Thank you.'

People applauded.

Seeing the person I saw next freaked me out—but not that much. I already knew, deep down, where the truth lay. This was just more confirmation that I was right and Mum and Doc Cousins were wrong.

I saw Mungo.

He didn't see me. He was manurely kitted out in nylon shorts and black socks with cheapo trainers, and was walking through the crowds and rain with his head held up as if it wasn't raining, as he had when I first saw him. Before I realized what I was doing I had raised my arm and called out, 'Mung—' I strangled the word in my throat and brought my arm down. He carried on walking—he hadn't seen or heard me—and I started to tail him.

Mungo reached the village hall and took the steps two at a time. I noticed a couple sitting on a bench to the left of the hall's open double doors, just below the Plunkett-Strawberry poster. I didn't recognize them at first. It wasn't that easy to see properly through the heavy rain, but it wasn't just the rain that made recognition difficult. The couple looked different, like imperfect replicants of themselves.

The couple were Mum and the Bozo.

The Bozo was balder and thinner, as if he was his own twin brother, while Mum was fatter. She was wearing clothes she wouldn't have been seen dead in usually, a semi-dead manure muncher's combo of pleated skirt, blouse with high frilly collar, and a pearl necklace. But her hair was the weirdest. Since this morning, on a day when Britain's first hurricane had trashed half of the south of England, closing down television stations and taking out power lines and phone masts, a hairdresser's had somehow managed to open for business as usual: Mum had had her hair cut into a horrible fringe and dyed blonde.

Then Mungo said the thing that proved I was right about the one thing in the world that I wished I wasn't right about. He said to Mum—*my* mum—'Hello, Mum.'

I stayed on the bottom step, feeling frozen to the spot. I could hear and see everything but there were enough people in the way for Mum, the Bozo, and Mungo not to be aware of me. Mum looked Mungo straight in the eye and said, 'Oh, hello, darling. We were wondering where you'd got to. Come and sit down.' The Bozo slid away from Mum along the bench and she patted the gap between them, saying, 'Dad's managed to wangle three camp beds for us in the hall so we should get a reasonable night's sleep. Did you find any bottled water?'

Mungo shook his head and sat down between Mum and the Bozo. They linked arms behind Mungo's back and shuffled up so the three of them turned into a squishy sandwich of family yuckiness. Mum put her hand right on Mungo's horrible, wet, mongy hair. Her fingers ran up and down his centre parting. The Bozo slapped Mungo's knee and said, 'I'd been *planning* to take you on a camping trip.' Then he laughed.

Mum said, 'Your father's full of it today. Our house may have just been flattened by a terrible storm—'

Mungo said, 'I would say the winds were above seventy-five mph, so that would make it an official hurricane.'

'—but all he can think about is being a Boy Scout again.'

Comprendee, Dad, why I was in the state I was in? In those two or three seconds of being betrayed, my heart hit the ground like a broken lift. The lift turned into a wolf tunnel and from the tunnel a wolf sprang, taking the village hall steps three at a time. The wolf's fur had that cappuccino swirl and he looked as if he was smiling, but he wasn't smiling, his dagger teeth were out and they were looking for a throat. I leapt at Mum. My hands went towards her shoulders and I yelled in her face, 'WHAT ARE YOU DOING?

223

WHAT ARE YOU DOING? YOU LIED TO ME, YOU LIED, YOU LIAR.'

My hands went right through her.

It was like dipping my hands in human-coloured water. Just a tickle as they disappeared into her shoulders. I pulled them out and they were intact again. I stared at my hands. I stared at Mum. I'd screamed as loudly as I could, ten centimetres from her face, and she hadn't reacted. She was still stroking Mungo's hair.

My lips were shaping into the M of Mum when she turned away from me, pulled Mungo into her arms and squeezed him tight. He screwed his head round to stare at me as she did this. I knew immediately he could see me because he tried to talk to me with his eyes, making them big and sad.

'Oh, darling,' Mum said from behind Mungo's head. 'You are the most precious thing to me in the whole wide world, you do know that don't you?' And when Mungo didn't reply she said, 'Don't you? Tell me you do.'

Mungo gave a tiny shake of the head, so tiny it was more a vibration than a shake, as if saying to me, 'What else can I say?'

Then he said to Mum, 'Yes, of course I do, Mum.'

# Chapter 17

The disappearing hands, the not being seen or heard—
I felt like a ghost in a nightmare. Half-running, half-
walking back along the Bickleigh Road—destination
unknown—I tried to think it through. But every
thought was like a clattering tube train heading for
the end of the line, and me strap-hanging as it picked
up speed towards High Barnet or Morden or Ealing
Broadway. At first I avoided the impact by jumping
from train to train, but there were too many thoughts,
too many trains, too much noise. They all hit the buf-
fers at the same time and burst into flames of horror:
I didn't exist any more.

Why not? Because I was dead.

Like Dad.

Mungo had killed me and taken over my life.

The ultimate scam.

I even thought I might see Dad coming the other
way, leopardskin creepers restored to full glory. Then
I'd fall into step alongside him and Dad would say,
'I hate grass, I hate trees—'

And I'd reply, 'Gimmee tattoo parlours and tower
blocks any day!'

And he'd look at me sideways, the way he did on the Heath when we were looking for the Two-Dimensional Tree (which incidentally, Dad, proves that you do like trees). We'd walk over the brow of the hill and there would be Whipsnade Wildlife Park down below. I'd point at signs saying 'Wolf Enclosure' and Dad'd ruffle my hair and say, 'Same old same old. Not so bad, this being dead caper, is it?'

But I didn't see Dad, just an empty road in the rain, strewn with storm damage. And I thought: this is what it is like to be dead. Everyone wonders what it is like and now I know. Walking an empty road in the rain, for ever. Simple really.

My heart leapt in my chest. I thought it was Dad calling me. 'Mungooo!' I turned and stared. Back down the road, a speck waved. But it was Mungo. I had no wolf-fight left. I stood like a sheep and waited for my murderer to catch me up. He ran through the rain, hurdling the junk on the road with his giraffe legs, and by the time he reached me he was out of breath. 'Are you all right? I can explain. We can—*wheeze*—get you out of this, I promise. OK?'

'You killed me,' I said. I felt quite calm as I said it but then, I couldn't help it, I burst into tears.

Mungo held out a hand but I backed off. 'Is that what you think?' he said. 'It's not as bad as that. You never read the book, did you?' And that was when he talked about the rain and the sudden drop in barometric pressure. 'Sometimes, in extreme weather conditions like we've had this summer, it happens—*cough*—so quickly it leaves a gap that you can slip through, into a parallel world. Provided, of course, you've got what Mungo Groves called the "radar", which—*wheeze*—we both must have because it's a dominant gene in the family—like our attached earlobes. But now you seem to have got stuck in the—'

I shook my head, understanding less than nothing of what he was saying.

'OK OK,' said Mungo. 'I'm going too fast for you. I'm sorry. The best thing to do is for you to come back home with me and we'll—'

'No way,' I said, and took a step back.

'You must,' said Mungo. 'You must see the book. Then you'll believe me. And then we have to work out what to do before it's too late.'

'You promise I'm not dead?' I said.

'Promise.'

I could have hugged him, even though I knew he was a liar.


The Pineapple House had shifted and slipped, like a sinking ship. At one end the battlements now sloped distinctly downwards. Standing in between the gate-posts, Mungo paused and stared. 'The house was built in eighteen eighty-eight,' he said. 'I thought it would stand for a thousand years but, it must have been about three a.m., it got sucked right into the vortex

227

of the depression. It felt like being in a plughole, with all this negative energy being sucked down on top of us. Scary, I can tell you. Things flying everywhere, like a family of poltergeists had moved in. We got out as soon as we could this morning.'

'We?' I said.

In reply he patted me on the back and said, 'Come on.'

'What happened to the bungalow?' I said.

'It was never built,' said Mungo. I stared at him. 'Don't worry, I'll explain.'

At the front door Mungo ripped down the notice that said

POLICE NOTICE
**UNSAFE STRUCTURE**
_DO NOT ENTER_

and slid the key into the lock. He turned the key and opened the door a fraction, then stopped and listened. The creaking and splintering of wood. The tinkling of broken glass. Mungo shrugged and eased the door fully open.

The Pineapple House felt like a lightbulb that was about to ping into oblivion. The slightest movement or raised voice might trigger a final disintegration. Downstairs, the hall ceiling had dropped at one end and hung by a few electric wires and splinters of joists. The light fitting swayed in a breeze that blew down two storeys through the shattered roof. The staircase that faced us had split in half and there was a gap of two metres between the seventh and eighth steps. From the doorway, Mungo pointed at the staircase and whispered, 'We need to be up there. Let's go easy, OK?'

I nodded.

We tiptoed past a row of wellies and a flash of the nightmare came back to me—a single, glistening drop of blood on green rubber. The wooden hall floor was sludgy with dust and rain. Mungo, going first, almost slipped over and his trainer squeaked on the slippery floor as he tried to regain his balance. I reached out to steady him—and feeling the texture of his T-shirt under my fingers I realized I was solid. I still existed! 'Hey,' I whispered.

Mungo stopped and turned his head. 'Yes?'

'Nothing.' I couldn't express it but I suddenly felt really choked and grateful to Mungo.

We made it to the stairs. The staircase shook as Mungo put his foot on the first step. He brought his other foot up and rocked on the step, testing it out. 'Best go one at a time,' he said. I watched him climb. The staircase continued to shake and creak, but seemed to be holding. When he reached the gap between the seventh and eighth steps, Mungo hesitated then extended his right leg across the gap. For a moment it looked as if he'd be stuck in the splits position but he managed to push his body forward and haul his trailing leg across.

Mungo reached the top and lay down on the

229

landing so his head and shoulders were hanging over the top step. Then he flicked his fingers, encouraging me to climb. As far as the seventh step was easy. I could feel the staircase swaying slightly under my feet but it felt solid enough. When I came to the gap, I jumped, hit the eighth step with my right foot, got a two-fingered grip on the banister and brought my left foot up. Then—it was the weight of both feet that did it—the step just broke off, fell away in a splintering sound beneath me, left me dangling from the banister by two fingers.

My legs swished in the void. The pressure on my fingers was growing at the speed of sound and I knew I was going to have to let go and crash down through the smashed and splintered wood. Then Mungo, transforming himself into a specialist belly-surfing unit of the Eighth Armoured Division, slid down the staircase on his front. As my fingers released their grip on the banister he grabbed my free arm just below the elbow and dragged me up the steps to safety. I crawled the rest of the way on to the landing and lay down on a red rug, staring up at a smashed ceiling that looked like ribs poking through skin.

'OK?' said Mungo.

'Close thing. Yeah. How are we going to get back down?'

'Plenty of time for that. We need to be in Mum's room. Over there.' He pointed at one of the closed doors. 'Mum and Dad have separate rooms.'

Mungo opened the door slowly and peered in. 'It's fine in here. Not even a crack in the ceiling.'

I followed him into the room.

It smelt of Mum, of smoothly sliding drawers full of folded silk. On the dressing table there were photographs in silver frames. Mum as a little girl, in plaits. Mum with five other little girls, holding a centipede outfit with huge eyes and lots of dangling false legs. Mum in a wedding dress outside a church, standing next to—

'I can't handle this,' I said.

Standing next to the Bozo. Getting married to the Bozo.

'If I'm not dead I must be a psycho,' I said. 'What's going on?'

'Neither,' muttered Mungo. 'Soon.' He'd opened the wardrobe door and got down on his knees to search inside. 'Mum doesn't know I go in here,' he said. 'It's where I found the cigarette lighter. Every so often I keep it out for a few days but I always put it back so she doesn't find it missing. Here.' He held an object over his shoulder. I took it: the old lighter with M. G. engraved on it in swirly old-fashioned writing. 'It stays with the book usually,' Mungo said. Now he was dragging out something big from the back of the wardrobe, tugging it through the piles of old clothes and sandals.

He patted the top of it and a puff of dust rose in the perfumed air. Then he turned and carried it over to the bed where he laid it carefully down. It was a large, thick, heavy-looking book in a torn cloth cover that

231

had once been blue but had faded to grey. I looked at Mungo. 'Be my guest,' he said.

I put the lighter in my pocket and opened the book. The pages were thick and yellow, with crinkly edges. As I turned them the book creaked like the straining wood of the damaged Pineapple House. The first page was blank. On the second page was written

### The Mysterious Cosmos
#### Sir Mungo Groves
#### Edinburgh 1947

I looked at Mungo. He nodded. 'Keep going,' he said. I turned to the next page.

'Read it,' said Mungo.

This is what I read:

*Is the cosmos a mere machine—no more mysterious than the internal combustion engine in a motor car—or is there something altogether more imaginative at work in the formulation of our phenomenal world?*

I stopped reading. 'It's by my great-grandfather, right?' I said. 'How come—'

'Hasn't your mum kept a copy? I wondered.'

'She said it gave Grandpa bad memories so he chucked it.'

'Did she explain about Mungo Groves?' said Mungo. I nodded but Mungo was determined to give me his own version. 'He was a very well known and respected astronomer and scientist in the nineteen thirties. Did you know there's a crater named after him on the moon? Groves Crater. He also had a big hand in inventing radar. Then in nineteen forty-seven he writes this book, *The Mysterious Cosmos*, and people think he's gone mad. They laugh at him. He loses his job. And eventually he really does go completely crazy. He died in a mental home in Scotland.'

'Why did they think he'd gone mad?'

'Because of what's in the book. He believed in the existence of simultaneous parallel realities. Not only that. Listen to this.' And Mungo leant over the book, flicked forward a couple of pages and read:

*Furthermore, I declare to the world for the first time that I have made the journey between such realities. I, Mungo Groves, have travelled successfully between parallel worlds.*

He tapped the page, stood upright and lifted his hands. His fingers trembled. Preacherman. Insects' wings. The strangest thing being, his fingers at those moments seemed to have a life of their own and I don't think he even knew what they were doing. He was looking me straight in the eyes and he was grinning. I felt a shiver run through me.

'Are you beginning to understand now?' said Mungo.

He went over to the dressing table and picked up the

framed photograph of Mum and the Bozo on their wedding day. 'My mum and dad,' he said.

'They can't be,' I said. 'Because that's *my* mum, whatever you say. You can't take that away from me.'

'Calm down,' said Mungo, 'don't get upset. You still don't get it, do you?'

'I don't know anything any more,' I admitted.

'Well, it's true, Clare is your mother. But she's also mine. You are the son your mother—our mother—would have had if she'd left the Bickleigh area at the age of nineteen and gone to London to a do a course in graphic design, and met your father.'

'Which she did.'

'Precisely. Of course she did.'

'So what are you saying?'

'Because she also didn't,' said Mungo. 'It's to do with what Mungo Groves shows in his book, about parallel possibilities. Mum also stayed in Bickleigh, and married my dad, whose name is Brian Boland, who she met at a Young Farmers' Club dance when she was sixteen. She told me it was touch and go whether she went to London in nineteen eighty-one. She'd already been offered a place so she went up to see the college for a day and it was the first time she'd ever been to London and she hated it. She came back and thought about it and decided she couldn't face three years of noise and pollution and dangerous characters lurking on every street corner so she stayed here, and four years later, after Dad had been to agricultural college, she and Dad got married in Bickleigh church—when this photo was taken—and went to live in Pineapple House, on the Bickleigh Road, where we are now, and I came along six years later.'

He put the photograph back on the dressing table. 'They look happy, don't they? But they probably weren't, even then. They've always rowed, for as long as I can remember, and I've always hated it. Even just now, by the village hall, all that hugging and making jokes, it's all put on. They can't stand each other. That's how this started, because I wanted to change. I wanted to be someone else. If only Mum hadn't married Dad, I thought. If only she'd picked another man to marry, then I'd still have Mum, and I'd still be sort of me, but things would be happier. And then I found this old book and I realized I could escape, I could make it come true.'

Mungo picked up the book. 'It's all in here,' he said and, finding a particular page, started to read.

*The world of space and time is like a thick primeval forest. Our lives feel like a path through the forest. But for every step we take in one direction, there is an infinite number of steps we could have taken in another direction—and indeed did take, albeit in a different, parallel reality. If we were able to view the entirety of these realities from the topmost branch of the tallest tree in the forest, we would see not a straight path but a dense pattern of endlessly branching and subdividing tracks spreading to fill that literally endless space.*

'See?' said Mungo. 'Take Clare Groves. Our mother. She goes to London, marries your dad and has you. One reality. Or she stays in Bickleigh, marries my dad,

235

and has me. Reality number two. One is not more real than the other. It's just that your reality feels like it's the only one because you don't have the ability to perceive or experience any others. Except now you do. I'm the other reality. How do you do?' Mungo grabbed my hand and shook it.

I still didn't understand, not fully, but I felt a glimmer, a stirring of wolf wisdom. I laughed, still feeling the relief of not being dead, and went all London. 'Hey, *dude*,' I said, right-handing Mungo's shoulder. 'How's it goin', yeah?'

'This book,' said Mungo, ignoring me, 'tells you how to make the journey between parallel realities. Mum mentioned it years ago but I'd forgotten. Then a couple of months ago when Mum and Dad had been arguing a lot and Dad had hit her and she had to go to the GP, I found it. I can't explain it but something made me search through her drawers and cupboards and there it was. I started reading, sitting here on Mum's floor and listening out for the sound of cars in the drive. And it was like climbing to the top of the tallest tree in the forest and looking down on my life.

'But it's not just the stuff about forests. It tells you *how*. It explains the gap between the worlds, how it only opens up at times of unusual barometric activity. How, when this happens, you have to find an environment that replicates, as far as possible, a place outside time and consciousness. He means darkness, quiet, no link to everyday life.' He flicked through the pages and read out another sentence from *The Mysterious Cosmos*.

*Imagine an enclosed space, entirely cut off from the outside world, analagous to the box containing that endlessly put-upon feline, Dr Schroedinger's Cat. In such a—*

'Schroedinger's the magician dude you mentioned, right?'

Mungo smiled. 'Schroedinger did this experiment. He put a cat in a box—well, he didn't really, he was just imagining it, but anyway . . . ' He saw me doing a cartoon yawn. 'The point is, he showed that the cat can exist in parallel realities at the same time. Well, Mungo Groves found his own box that was completely cut off from the world, but he didn't put a cat in it, he put himself in it. His box was the cellar of an old house in Edinburgh, and that's what made me think of the well. I'd played in the Happy Valley house a few times so I knew about it. My problem was, there was no one to take away the rope ladder for me.' He laughed and looked towards the window. 'I haven't exactly got millions of friends. So, when I was down the well I wasn't "entirely cut off from the outside world" as Sir Mungo said you have to be. But it worked anyway. I think my genes are predisposed, like our great-grandfather's were. He called it "the radar".

'It was the radar that told me about you, I reckon. I didn't know what was happening. I started getting this noise in my head, like a badly tuned radio. I knew something—or someone—had moved nearby and I had to find it, or them, or whatever it was. So I did. I made sure the atmospheric conditions were right and it worked so well for me I floated right into your reality the very first time I tried it. I turned up outside the kitchen window of your cottage and there you were, in a red dressing gown—'

'Arsenal,' I said.

'I saw you through the window, eating a bacon sandwich. And your mum—our mum—was there and you looked really happy together. The next stage was to bring you back into my reality. And that worked too, as the book said it would. I couldn't believe it was so simple. That was the first time we saw each other, when I was walking through the rain. Of course I saw you but I was so amazed and nervous I couldn't think what to say, so I pretended I hadn't noticed you. Next time, we talk and you tell me about your father, what a good dad he is—so different from mine—and that's when I knew.'

'Knew what?'

Mungo hesitated. 'Look, I'm really sorry. I was desperate.' He paced around the room and went to the window. Staring out at trees shaking and bending in the hurricane's coat tails, he said, 'I've got a confession to make.'

# Chapter 18

Mungo went back to the bed and picked up the book.

*In such a space,* he read, then paused: '—he means his cellar in Edinburgh, or down the well—anywhere that's cut off from the outside world—'

*In such a space, when mind and matter are fluid, I maintain it is possible to exchange minds but preserve matters. In the right circumstances, and with a subject who is genetically equipped with what I have referred to elsewhere as 'the radar', this may be achieved entirely by the power of thought.*

Mungo closed the book and pushed it across Mum's bed. 'I liked your life,' he said. 'I liked the way you looked and dressed. You knew all about London. I mean, wow!, the great metropolis. I've hardly been out of Bickleigh.'

I laughed at this. 'But you said—'

Mungo carried on talking. 'You loved your mum and dad and they loved you, I could feel that. I thought we could swap. The book says it can happen if you want it enough. And I really did want it. Mum and Dad had just had their worst row ever. They were talking about splitting up and who did I want to live with, her or him? I just wanted to escape. That's why I—' Mungo hesitated. 'Promise you won't go crazy when I tell you?' he said. He was remembering the time he had stirred up the wolf. I didn't react. I was still as stone. Mungo cleared his throat and spoke quickly.

'That's why I brought you into my reality, sent you down the well and took the rope ladder away, if you want to know. When I sent the rope ladder back down and you came up, you were supposed to have turned into me and I was supposed to have turned into you.'

I stared at him.

'My mind would take over your body, your life. And you would take over mine. But the thing is, you would never know. As the book says,'—he looked down at the page—'"this may be achieved without the consent or knowledge of the person whose mind and body are being thus separated and exchanged".' He started pacing again. 'But I know that's no excuse,' he said, without looking at me.

I thought of the nightmare, the inescapable feeling that the Bozo was my father. Mungo's plan had almost worked, I realized. I had been within a Rizla paper's width of becoming bloody Mungo, complete with centre parting and a sicko bozo for an old man. I couldn't believe what he was telling me. 'You'd have just stolen my life?' I said, forgetting to whisper.

'I was unhappy!' Silence. The sound of falling rain

and creaking timbers. 'Anyway,' said Mungo, 'it didn't work did it? Nothing happened.'

And then I realized. 'Yeah,' I said, 'it did actually.' In my head I did a mini Arsenal goal celebration with myself. I'd scammed him back and I didn't even know it! I told him about the nightmare I'd had down the well of being in the Pineapple House and seeing his dad hit his—my—mum. 'There was bright red blood on his welly. It was horrible. And then I was convinced that the—your dad—was my dad. And then, and then—'

But I didn't tell him the next bit, about how Dad, my real dead dad, had swum into my thoughts just in time. Dad had saved me! And that was our secret, his and mine.

'—and then I woke up,' I continued. 'I didn't tell you about the dream because it freaked me out and because I didn't want to give you the satisfaction of being right. Anyway, there was one slight technical problem with your plan.'

'What?' said Mungo, looking surprised. He thought he'd covered everything.

'My dad died in February.'

Outside, roof tiles were still slipping and crashing. Then a deafening, splintering noise like a clap of thunder that shook the whole house, followed by a loud bang above us in the roof space. We flinched, expecting the ceiling to collapse. Everything went quiet again and we stared at each other.

Mungo said, 'But you didn't—' He put his head in his hands. 'Your dad is dead,' he mumbled through his fingers. 'I never thought of that. I'm really sorry.'

'*De nada*,' I said. A dad saying, another one. You could make a book out of his sayings.

Then Mungo lifted his face and smiled. 'Anyway, guess what, it's worked out anyway because—' He hesitated again. It wasn't like Mungo to be stuck for words.

'Because what?' I said.

'We're friends,' he said, and turned his head towards the window.

'Hey,' I whispered, 'you know what my dad'd say about all this, if he was alive?'

'What?'

'"Laugh? I nearly shat".'

'What does that mean?'

'Never mind. The point is, what's happened to me and how do I get out of it?'

No reply. Mungo was still facing the window and seemed to be staring at something many miles away.

'Mungo?' I said. 'For God's sake. I'm practically a ghost. Even my own mum can't see or feel me. I can't be a ghost for ever.' Then I got suspicious. 'You're not trying to scam me again, are you? This is not more Mungo bullshit?'

He seemed to ignore me, and when he spoke it was as if to himself. 'It should be simple. In theory.'

'What should?'

'You're stuck in my reality, you know that? The book does warn it can happen. The weather's the last straw. The barometric pressure has never been lower. Things have gone haywire. People are probably leaking from reality to reality all over the place, if we could

242

only see them, if we could only climb that tall tree and look down on the forest of our lives.

'But something else has been going on here too, and I was so stupid I missed it. You're just as unhappy as me, aren't you?'

'Not so's I've noticed,' I said.

'Yes you are. I was so wrapped up in my own unhappiness I didn't see yours. I hate my dad and you've just lost yours. Neither of us want to be who we are and that is not a good idea. All sorts of things can go wrong with these experiments in parallel worlds when you don't like yourself. People can get permanently stuck between realities. The ones who really don't know who they are. They just spin endlessly in nowhere, like a washing machine that never reaches the end of its cycle. Mungo Groves warns about that.'

'So what are you saying?'

'You're stuck because you don't know who you are or who you want to be. But the answer is simple. We go back to the well. You go down to the bottom and I take the rope ladder away. You go into a dream and when you wake up the rope ladder will be there again. You climb back up the rope ladder and you'll be back in the reality you want to be in. There's just one problem.'

'What?'

'You have to know—to really know—who and where you want to be. Otherwise you could end up nowhere. Do you know yourself? I mean *really* know?'

'Of course,' I said, but my heart was thu-thumping.

'What's the answer?'

243

'Mungo McFall. Two thousand and six. Bickleigh.' That last word was difficult to say. To actually choose to be in Manuresville rather than, say, Camden or Barbados!

But the next thought was a million times harder. Mungo said, 'What about your dad?'

'What about him?'

'You have to accept that he's dead.'

I swallowed. 'I do,' I said.

'OK,' said Mungo, 'I just hope you really know your head and your heart. Otherwise—'

'Where will *you* be?' I said, hoping he'd still be around to help me out if it all went pear-shaped.

'I'll be gone for ever from your world, and you'll be gone for ever from mine. That's how it has to be.'

Mungo replaced *The Mysterious Cosmos* at the bottom of the wardrobe. 'You know something?' he said. 'Maybe this isn't such a good book after all. People should just be happy with who and where they are and get on with it, don't you think? They shouldn't always think that somebody else is happier than they are. Have you still got the lighter?' I handed it back and he leant forward to replace it in the wardrobe. Then he said to himself, 'On second thoughts . . . ' and put the lighter in his pocket

We went out on to the landing. The staircase had disappeared—the reverberating crash we'd heard minutes earlier. Just the top step remained, a step to nowhere. We looked down at the smashed stairs, strewn in piles of brick and broken, splintered wood across the hall floor five metres below. 'Think you can make it?' said Mungo.

The problem wasn't just the height but the junk and rubble, which could do you a nasty injury if you landed awkwardly. 'Isn't there another staircase?' I said.

Mungo shook his head. 'But I know what there is,' he said. 'Wait here.' He disappeared through another bedroom door. I heard bashing and banging as drawers were opened and closed. Then Mungo was standing there dangling a long purple elastic contraption that looked like a parachute harness. 'Dad's braces,' he said. 'I hate it when I'm with him and he's wearing them.'


On our way to the Happy Valley I admitted I had known Mungo's dad in my reality, and that I had nicknamed him the Bozo, partly because once when I saw him he had been wearing a thing called a cravat. Mungo didn't mind because he didn't like his dad and, anyway, as he said, what happened in my reality shouldn't be any of his business.

Then Mungo explained why the Pineapple House was a bungalow sometimes—in my reality, the Pineapple House was derelict and was finally demolished in the early nineteen seventies. A bungalow was built in its place but the white wall and the gateposts with the pineapples were left as they were.

It was a similar story with Hedge End Hall House, aka the Happy Valley House. I explained to Mungo that in my world his father, Brian Boland, had not married Clare Groves but a woman called Felicity and had a daughter called Talullah. They had bought the derelict Hedge End Hall House and grounds and set up a battery chicken farm and agricultural plant hire business there. In Mungo's world, the house and grounds had remained derelict and were nicknamed the Happy Valley.

'And so it goes on,' said Mungo. 'As *The Mysterious Cosmos* says, it's "a dense pattern of endlessly branching and subdividing tracks". As far as you know, the village shop is run by the smelly chap, but to me it's the queer—'

'Gay. Please. For God's sake, Mungo.'

The driveway to the Happy Valley House was completely flooded. We sloshed along knee-deep in muddy rainwater. The gargoyles had never been so noisy, we heard them from about a kilometre away. But the old house didn't look damaged at all. In the courtyard at the back of the house we retrieved the rope ladder, dragged it over to the well and tied one end to the rusty ring in the ground. I tugged on the knot. It seemed secure. Mungo fed the other end of the rope ladder over the lip of the well. 'Right then,' he said. 'This is it. We won't see each other again. We must make the best of what we've got.'

'Cool.' I held up the palms of my hands for him to high-five them.

'What are you doing?'

'Don't you know? Forget it.'

'Good luck then. And remember: know who you are.' He shook my hand as if we were two elderly manure munchers about to zoom off in our manure-powered coffins.


I climbed down till Mungo's head was just a blur in the pale, squashed circle of light far above. Then, steadying myself with my left hand, I lifted my right and gave a small wave. I was glad I was so far down that Mungo couldn't see the tear I felt roll down my cheek and turn to salt on my lip. I waited for him to wave back. Nothing. Then, just as I'd given up hope, he raised both hands. A belated high five. I grinned and sniffed in the dark and cold as his face finally slipped from view.

Down, down I went, taking it slowly so I didn't scrape my knuckles on the sides, trying to remember all of Mungo's advice as I went. When I got to the bottom I had to give a sharp tug on the rope ladder and he would pull it up. Then I had to make myself comfortable on the bottom of the well, close my eyes and try to empty my mind. In theory, scenes and images from my reality should start to rush in, but if they didn't, I was to will them into being.

Most important of all, I mustn't be tempted into wishing for unrealistic things. I just had to want to be

247

me, Mungo McFall. And slowly, without even noticing, as easily as falling asleep, I would slip back into
my own reality. The process wasn't to be rushed.
Mungo reckoned he hadn't waited long enough last
time, so now he would wait at least fifteen minutes
before lowering the rope ladder back down. When I
opened my eyes, all I had to do was climb back up and
Mungo McFall's world would be waiting for me at
the top.


When I reached the bottom I didn't think anything of
the water at first. There was about five or six centimetres, enough to cover my trainers when I stepped
off the rope ladder, but after all the rain there'd been
it didn't surprise me that some had got into the well.
I had more important things to think about, such as:
how well did I know my own mind?

I planted my feet apart in the cold water and leant
against the damp chalk of the well side with one arm
looped round a slimy rung of the rope ladder. Silence.
The darkness was grey and suffocating. When I moved
my feet, the water in the bottom of the well plinked
around my ankles. Slowly, my ears tuned into another
sound, from higher up. The dripping of water. I wanted
to call up to Mungo, to hear his voice one last time,
but I resisted the temptation. Time to do what I had
to do. I tugged on the rope ladder. No reaction. I
tugged harder, and the rope ladder jerked under my
grasp and slithered up and away. I listened till the

slithering sound stopped, which meant the ladder had reached the top. I imagined Mungo coiling it up and carrying it back to the storage room behind the stack of roof tiles. I imagined Mungo walking away for ever. I felt very lonely in those moments, engulfed by the great silence of the well bottom. Not quite silence: the sound of dripping water was still there and if anything seemed louder, more insistent than before.

This was it. I squeezed my eyes tight shut and thought about my world and how much I wanted to be in it again. My mum, of course. Even Bickleigh, even The Hollow, even the Bozo shagging my mum and snotfaced Talullah being my best friend if that's what it took. Just let me be Mungo McFall!

My beating heart was drumming me to sleep. When I woke, would I be me or would I be nowhere?

# Chapter 19

The first thing I noticed was that the water level had risen. The sounds of dripping water had joined up into a trickle, water was now seeping steadily into the well and had already reached up to my knees. Second thing I noticed: no rope ladder. Mungo had not sent it back down even though fifteen minutes had surely elapsed. I called up the cold and empty tube of the well: 'Mungooo!'

I suddenly felt icy cold. This surely was my new reality. I hadn't reclaimed Mungo McFall's life. I'd become a kid trapped down a well, end of story. Not quite end of story. At this rate, the end of the story would be me drowning.

Sudden, deafening noise. A loud metallic clanging from high above, like a high-security prison door sliding shut, followed by a pitch blackness that made the greyness of before seem as bright as floodlights. Imagine being mummified in bubblewrap, gaffer-taped in black binbags, thrown in the nose-cone of a rocket and fired into outer space. That's how dark and lonely it suddenly felt. Another noise: chickens. The squawking of hundreds and hundreds of battery chickens landing on my head like a shower of red-hot needles. If you wanted to send someone mad in five seconds, you would play them a recording of this sound.

Then the well turned into the belly of a rattlesnake. A reverberating rattle that started at the top and echoed downwards until something hit me on the head and I lost my footing and staggered over into the water, copping a mouthful. 'Euurggh!' I spluttered and floundered around, trying to regain my balance, and as I did so my hand found and grabbed on to something. The rope ladder.

*Calma, calma.* The trickling sounds had joined up into a steady stream. The water was up to my middle now—I stood on tiptoes as it flickered and teased around my belly button. But that didn't matter. Neither did the incessant, maddening squawking nor the throb on my forehead where a rung of the ladder had whacked me. All that mattered was that I was still me and I had my means of escape. I steadied the ladder, found the bottom rung with my right foot, and started to climb.

As I climbed, I felt happier, lighter, with each step. Not far now, and I would slither out into a life that had never seemed so desirable. I was so excited I didn't even notice that there was no light coming from the top of the well. Then, over the squawking, came a voice, surprisingly close.

'Mungo?' shouted the voice. 'It's Mungo. Change of plan. I'm coming down.'

At that moment the sole of Mungo's trainer landed on my head. I reached up and grabbed his ankle. 'It's me,' I shouted back. 'I'm right underneath you. Get out of my way, Mungo. I've had enough of all this. I just want to go home.'

'You can't,' he said. 'We've got to go to the bottom. It's the only way.'

'We'll drown down there. It's filling up with water. I don't know what scam you're pulling now but just let me past.'

There we were, frozen in blackness like spiders in a drain. A thousand chickens squawking, four lungs wheezing, two hearts thumping. Waiting for something to happen, for one of us to give way.

'Listen,' said Mungo eventually, 'you have to trust me.'

'Ha!' I said. 'I've heard that before.'

'The well is blocked off. Can't you see? That's why there's no light. In your reality it's been covered over and it sounds like that battery chicken barn you mentioned has been built over the top. You can't get out, Mungo. That's what I'm trying to say. I could have left you. This is your reality, not mine. I'm running a big risk being here. But when I realized what had happened I had to try and help you.'

I didn't say anything. It was the no-choice choice. D'you wanna die or d'you wanna die? I squeezed Mungo's ankle and headed back to my watery tomb.


The water was tickling my armpits. Mungo, who was about ten centimetres taller than me, said, 'Here. Stand on my feet.'

I felt Mungo's cold breath on my face when he spoke. But we couldn't see each other. We had our arms around one another, for balance and to keep warm. But I was still freezing. My legs were going numb. After a while, Mungo had to hold me under the arms to keep me from slipping into the water. That's all I wanted to do really, to slip away, into unconsciousness. But Mungo kept me talking.

'What was your dad like?' he said. 'Apart from being nice.'

'Cool,' I said. 'He was cool. Had . . . ' I felt myself going.

'What did he have, Mungo?'

'Cool footwear. Leopardskin creepers.' I laughed. 'You wouldn't look cool in them. Hey, this is my reality, right? So what are you doing here?'

'I couldn't just leave you, could I?'

The water was past my chin. I had to tilt my head back to stop it going in my mouth. There wasn't much time left. 'What are we gonna do?' I said.

Silence. This time Mungo had no answers.

# Chapter 20

It was two days before they found me. My vital signs were barely flickering, that's what the fireman who dragged me through the tunnel and into the cellar told Mum. The water had drained off by then and he found me slumped on the bottom of the well. They reckoned some life-force in me kept my body upright for long enough to survive. I didn't tell them otherwise. I didn't tell them anything.

Mum told me it was Tally the Tart who had the idea of looking in the cellar. Tally said the idea had just come to her, out of nowhere, but nobody believed that. Mum thought Tally and I had been secret mates who had been exploring in the cellar before and found the secret tunnel that leads to the bottom of the well. It's where smugglers used to hide contraband brandy in the eighteenth century and was easy enough to find out about. You just had to read Plunkett-Strawberry's pamphlet on the subject, on sale in all good antiquarian coffin emporiums.

Anyway, Mum told me what happened. They were sitting round the fire in Hedge End Hall House, apparently. 'They' were Mum, Brian (I must remember to call him that), Felicity, and Talullah. They were all worried sick, on the edge of their seats, Mum said. It was two days since I'd disappeared.

The mobile phone networks were down but the police had managed to check out people in London and eliminate the possibility that I had escaped up there again—though, as Mum said, how would I have got there, as the transport system was paralysed too? Teams of coppers with sniffer dogs had then spent a day combing the fields and woods around Bickleigh. Maybe I was trapped under a fallen tree (or drowned in a pond, which they didn't say out loud). While all this was going on, Brian and Felicity (see, I'm getting the hang of it) had put Mum up at Hedge End Hall House, which had been strong enough to withstand the hurricane—the only damage, apart from a few lost roof tiles, was to a couple of gargoyles—and has its own generator.

By the second day it looked as if all possibilities had been exhausted, and Mum said she had given up hope of ever seeing me alive again. Brian had lit a fire and they were all drinking tea and not saying anything, then Tally burst into the room all excited. Mum said she'd been very sweet and concerned all along and now she said, 'Why don't we look in the cellar?'

The Bozo—sorry, Brian—said, 'What are you talking about?'

Tally said, 'You know, the cellar.' She stamped on the floor. 'There's a secret tunnel down there, isn't there? I just have the strongest feeling that that's where he is.'

Felicity said, 'I didn't know we had a secret tunnel.'

Brian said, 'Please, Talullah, if you have to say something make sure it's sensible.'

'I mean it,' said Tally.

'Think about it, darling,' said Brian. 'Why would Mungo go into our cellar and find a secret tunnel? He wouldn't even know it was there. Not even your mother knew it was there.'

Mum said that Tally was smiling. 'Maybe he didn't go into the cellar,' she said, 'maybe he got there from the well.'

Tally left the room. Nobody said anything. The clock ticked on the mantelpiece. Five minutes later Tally was back, yelling, 'I can hear someone moaning! Call the fire brigade!'

They let me stay at Hedge End Hall House because the hospitals were full to overflowing with victims of the hurricane. After a doctor had checked me out, a nurse arrived with a saline drip and put a line into a vein in the back of my hand which had to stay in for twenty-four hours. I regained consciousness after a couple of hours. Not for the first time, I thought I'd died. I didn't recognize the room, and Mum was standing with her back to the window, so her head was back-lit and angelic looking. She leant down and hugged me and said, 'Oh, love, you're awake.'

And I knew I wasn't dead, I was back to being Mungo McFall. But the relief didn't last long. As I remembered details of those last few minutes before

I lost consciousness, the question became: who and where was Mungo Boland?

'What happened?' I said.

And that was when Mum explained about Tally and the rescue. 'All that time you were pretending you hated the very idea of her and you were secret friends!' Mum said. 'What a strange and wonderful boy you are.'

None of this made any sense at all. I shook my head. 'So when I was found,' I said, 'there wasn't—' I hesitated.

'Yes?' said Mum.

'—anyone with me?'

'Like who? Mungo, are you telling me there's somebody else missing out there? Because if so we need to tell the police straight away.'

Mum was already halfway to the door. 'No, no,' I said hurriedly. And then I said, very quietly—guiltily, too—'I only meant, you know, the person I mentioned before.'

'You mean Mungo? Oh, love.'

*Psy-cho! Psy-cho!* is what Mum was thinking.

She came over to the bed and hugged me for a long time. 'Promise me,' she said into my hair, 'however desperate or sad or lonely you get, you will never pull a trick like that again.'

My skin had turned white and wrinkly and I looked like a freak. But there was no permanent damage. Over the next two days I didn't see anybody except

Mum. She would bring in food and drink, help me to the loo if I needed to go, then just sit on the end of the bed chatting, but being careful not to talk about the really serious things that we both knew we would have to talk about eventually, when I was strong enough. Which was basically Dad dying and me being a psycho. On the whole, I preferred the idea of being a psycho, the idea that everything to do with Mungo was the product of my overripe and deranged imagination. I even tried to believe it. But the evidence was against me.

I knew straight away where I was, of course I did. After Mum had explained we were at Hedge End Hall House, which belonged to Brian and Felicity, I'd worked it out quite quickly. I was in the Happy Valley house. The fireplace in my bedroom, which had a vase of dried flowers in it and didn't look as if it had been used for years, was one of the fireplaces that had looked as if it was hanging in mid-air. The door of the room was in one of the doorways that had opened on to nothingness. But the Happy Valley house wasn't in my reality, I knew that now. I knew that Mungo had been telling the truth, that he had saved my life, and that now he was quite possibly spinning in nowhere, like a sock in a Bosch.

Once, from the far side of the house, I heard the twang and reverb of an electric guitar, followed by a heavy riff that sounded like a train. Tally, according to Mum. 'But I thought she played the cello,' I said.

'You thought lots of things,' said Mum, and winked. She was standing by the window looking out at the dark green trees and the drizzle that hung in them. 'Come here and give me a hug.'

We stood side by side at the window. Beyond Mum's head, the wolf gargoyle was visible. Its ears were back and it was spouting an endless twist of water. 'How would you feel if we went back to London?' she said, not looking at me.

'Yea-eah!' I jigged up and down, did the Arsenal goal celebration with myself.

'Glad that idea meets with approval then.'

'You're not scamming me?'

'I'm not scamming you, love. I think we put our time in Bickleigh down to experience and move on. I've become a believer in moving on.'

I felt cool—but guilty. Suddenly my life was looking brilliant while Mungo, who had saved it, was quite possibly rotating in nowhere. How would I ever know what had happened to him?

Mum squeezed me tight. 'How could you have thought your dad wasn't your real dad, eh? You're so like him it's not true. What was it he used to say? "I hate the country. I hate trees." And then what? "Gimme—"'

'Tower blocks. And kebab shops and tattoo parlours and bootleg vinyl stores and . . . and—'

'How are you feeling about him?'

'Cool,' I said, and Mum frowned, not believing me. 'Honest. I know he'll always be around in his own way

259

and that's all that matters. Hey, I can make you the Thai green curry at last. You can't get the ingredients round here. And I'll pay you back that dosh I took. Sorry about that.'

'*De nada*,' Mum said, and we both smiled.

'It's funny, you know,' said Mum, 'but I almost never left Bickleigh. When I was eighteen I got a place on a foundation course in London and I went up for the day to look at the college and I hated it. I'd hardly been to London before and it terrified me. Dodgy-looking characters on every street corner. I came back and told your grandma, no way was I living there. You never knew what might happen in a place like that. Huh!'

'Really?' I said, feigning surprise.

'Anyway, I'm glad to say that your grandpa persuaded me to give it a go, and of course I loved it. And I met your father and the rest is history.' She sniffled.

'It won't be like it used to be, mind, when we go back to London. For a start, I've no idea where we'll be able to afford. We may have to live further out, you do understand that, don't you, love?'

'I know that. We can start again. I'll make new mates, I don't mind.'

'We can go to Whipsnade one day if you like. See the wolves. I'll take you there.'

I shook my head. 'Nah,' I said.

'No?' Mum looked surprised.

'I've become a believer in moving on,' I said, and Mum pretended to hit me on the head for being cheeky.

'Well anyway,' she said, 'you can still see Vernon and Barry. I've forgotten all that business now. It was quite funny actually. You boys, I don't know.' She laughed.

'I don't think I want to see them. They'll never be like—' I was going to say 'Mungo'. 'Vern is a real maniac,' I went on. 'You wouldn't believe the things he does. Once he—'

Mum covered her ears. 'I don't want to know.'

'OK OK,' I said and Mum uncovered her ears. Then I said, 'So what about you and—you know . . .' I jerked my head towards the door, meaning the person whose house this was.

Mum made her eyes big, warning me not to speak too loudly, and said, 'Who? Oh, you mean the *BOZO*!'

And we both started giggling.

Then Mum shook her head, closed her eyes and said, 'What was I thinking of? Will you forgive me?'

'It's cool,' I said. 'You know what I've learned this summer? That the world is like a—' I pretended to search for the right word. '—like a forest, and a person's life is like a path through the forest. You think of it as a straight line but at every step you take there are loads of other steps you could take. So—' I couldn't remember how it went on.

Mum frowned. 'Where did you get that from? It sounds familiar.'

'Oh . . . er . . . it's something Dad used to say.'

'Anyway, go on,' said Mum, 'I'm listening. It's very interesting.'

'Oh, I can't remember,' I said. 'So Elvis might be hiding behind the next tree. That'll do.'

'Very profound, I'm sure,' she said.

On the third morning of my recovery, Tally poked her head round the door. It was the first time I'd seen her close up and she was completely different from how I thought she'd look. Her blonde hair had strange bits and pieces tied into it—ribbon, string, a button—and her heavy, black-rimmed glasses were sharp and cool, not swot-like at all. She was wearing baggy, faded denim dungarees. I pretended to be asleep while studying her through slit eyes. Her shoulders looked tensed. I imagined my hands on them. The tops of her arms would be bird-like, biscuit-like—hard and fragile at the same time.

After a minute I opened my eyes properly and said, 'Hello.'

She said, 'How ya feelin'? I been trying to get in to see you but your mum's been like on bodyguard duty all the time?'

I was amazed. She sounded very London. 'Oh right,' I said. 'Hey, thanks for—you know.'

Tally laughed and said, 'Hey, no problem.' Then she started whispering. 'Listen, I haven't told the full story to the police and the saddo otherwise known as my dad. I met a mate of yours and he asked me to give you a secret message? Said he was called Mungo? I didn't get that cos I thought *you* were called Mungo but hey it's probably a boy thing . . . Anyway,

262

he says to tell you he's cool. Well, he didn't use that word but that's what he meant.' She saw my expression and said, 'Don't worry, I really haven't told anyone. He said best not to, cos like your mum really hates him?'

'Right,' I said. I felt happiness and relief flooding through my body like sunshine across fields. Mungo was alive! Mungo was cool! At that moment nothing else mattered, not even my dad dying. I felt as if I could be happy for ever. 'Where . . . er . . . did you see him?' I said, staying dead calm on the outside.

'Oh, wow, it was really scary, right? I was playing guitar in my room and I didn't hear him come in and he like totally freaked me, I thought he was a ghost . . . '

And this was how I found out how Mungo saved my life. He told Tally he didn't normally break into people's houses but this was an emergency because his friend was seriously ill down the well. They'd gone in there from under the chicken barn and then the well started to flood and they couldn't get out. His mate fell unconscious and he thought they were both going to drown. Then, at the last second—he said he was just fiddling about, trying anything, he was that desperate—he found that hole in the floor of the well, and in the hole was a ring. He pulled the ring and a trapdoor opened into the secret smugglers' tunnel that leads to the cellar of Tally's house. While the rainwater was draining off from the well, Mungo had come up from the cellar to get help. Tally went down to the cellar, heard me moaning and rushed up yelling, 'Call 999!'

'He'd disappeared by then,' said Tally. 'Just vanished. Said he couldn't hang around, he had a long long way to get back. The way he said it, it was like he lived at the North Pole or something. Hey, is it true you're a trainspotter?'

'What!' I said. 'No way! Jesus! Who told you that?'

Tally shrugged, twisting the ribbon in her hair round her finger. Then she pointed at me and laughed. 'Wind up, wind up! Had you going, didn't I?'

The door opened and Mum came into the room. 'Oh sorry—' she said.

'It's OK,' said Tally. 'I was just going.'

'Before you do,' said Mum, 'I was just thinking, Tally. Perhaps, when Mungo and I have moved back to London, you'd like to come and stay with us?'

'Cool,' said Tally.

'Mungo? What d'you think?'

'Whatever,' I said, but my eyes were shining.

Tally walked to the door and put her hand on the doorknob. Then she turned back to face us. 'Oh yeah, nearly forgot,' she said. Her fingers fished around in the bib pocket of her dungarees. 'You know that guy I was just telling you about, who's called Mungo too?' She winked at me and produced a metallic object which she threw on the bed. 'He asked me to give you this.'

Nigel Richardson is the author of three previous books, *Breakfast in Brighton*, *Dog Days in Soho*, and *The Wrong Hands*, which was published to much acclaim in 2005. He was the deputy travel editor of *The Daily Telegraph* for 13 years and still writes for newspapers. He has also written several plays, a drama series, and a documentary series for BBC Radio 4. He was born in the Midlands, grew up in Yorkshire and Sussex, and lives in south-west London. He is a big fan of dogs and of Wolverhampton Wanderers FC. *The Rope Ladder* is his second novel for Oxford University Press.